"It's an interesting problem, isn't it?"

Blaize sat down beside Oriel as he continued. "We need the close affection, the comradeship, the interaction with our fellows, yet deep in most people's hearts there's resentment at the ties and responsibilities—the demands made on us by those we love."

"An interesting dichotomy," she said, a sly note of humor in her tone.

He laughed, appreciating her amusement. "Very interesting. I'm sure that's why the romance pedlars, those who say that one man and one woman can live happily ever after, are doomed to failure. Love begins in dependence and it ends in resentment and the struggle to be free."

"That is horribly cynical!" she exclaimed.

He raised an eyebrow in inquiry. "Waiting for your prince, Oriel?"

ROBYN DONALD lives in northern New Zealand with her husband and children. They love the outdoors and particularly enjoy sailing and stargazing on warm nights. Robyn doesn't remember being taught to read, but rates reading as one of her greatest pleasures, if not a vice. She finds writing intensely rewarding and is continually surprised by the way her characters develop independent lives of their own.

Books by Robyn Donald

Don't miss any of our special offers. Write to us at the following address for information on our newest releases.

Harlequin Reader Service
P.O. Box 1397, Buffalo, NY 14240
Canadian address: P.O. Box 603,
Fort Erie, Ont. L2A 5X3

ROBYN DONALD

a summer storm

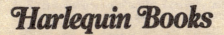

Harlequin Books

TORONTO • NEW YORK • LONDON
AMSTERDAM • PARIS • SYDNEY • HAMBURG
STOCKHOLM • ATHENS • TOKYO • MILAN

Harlequin Presents first edition November 1991
ISBN 0-373-11408-7

Original hardcover edition published in 1990
by Mills & Boon Limited

A SUMMER STORM

CHAPTER ONE

ORIEL RADFORD huddled into a chair; outside the world was drenched, battered by a cyclonic storm all the way from the tropics, but inside it was warm and dry. Her exhausted eyes surveyed what the housekeeper had called the morning-room. A somewhat old-fashioned term, she thought vaguely, for a comfortable, very pleasant living-room.

Even with a blanket slung around her shoulders she was unable to repress the shivers that racked her long body. Muddy water dripped from lank black curls on to the towel around her neck, she knew her lips were blue, and every bone in her body ached with deep-seated persistence. Thin fingers trembled as they gingerly explored one high cheekbone, and she winced at the swelling; she hesitated, then as carefully as she could investigated her throbbing temple. The same rock had bruised both her cheekbone and the side of her head; she had hit it when she had fallen into a hole as she forced her way through bush towards the beach.

A pale attempt at a smile touched her wide, soft mouth. Clumsy, as her mother was always saying.

She had read somewhere that the body could only cope with so much pain; after a certain amount no more was felt. Clearly she hadn't yet got there. Without even trying she could feel her foot, a sullen ache that peaked in a distinct sharp crescendo every time she moved it.

Not too far away a deep masculine voice with an in-built note of authority spoke incisively into a telephone. She lifted heavy eyelids and stared across the shadowed room. He was big, about six feet three, she estimated now, and very powerful. Oriel knew just how strong he was, for when she had collapsed in front of him on the beach about ten minutes ago those strong arms had lifted her and without any visible effort carried her into the house.

Another rigour shook her thin frame. His voice came nearer. 'Right,' he said crisply. 'That's Civil Defence informed, they'll organise a helicopter to get your companion out. Now, I'll carry you up to the bath my housekeeper should have ready for you.'

'Will they know where David is?'

He bent to pick her up, ignoring her tiny involuntary flinch. 'Yes, your directions were very explicit, and the pilot knows the Bay like his own back yard.'

Numbly, she nodded. 'I hope they find him soon.' The heavy lids, that even when she was wide awake and alert gave her a disconcertingly sulky air, drooped over her slanting, lack-lustre eyes, their normally dense blue washed almost completely from them.

She hadn't been embarrassed when he'd carried her into the house, but she was now. In spite of her effort to appear calm and collected, her stiff body betrayed her inner uneasiness. Somehow, in some dim region of herself that still functioned in spite of her weariness, the first faint tendrils of fear uncurled. Ludicrous though it was, she felt threatened.

He negotiated the door with a lithe grace that seemed unusual for such a big man, but again, there were no signs of undue exertion. Such strength was somehow unnerving.

The muscles of his big body bunched and flowed against her. She was too aware of a faint scent teasing her nostrils. The secret, intimate perfume of masculinity, she deduced, arousing and endlessly fascinating. It was blatant sexual magnetism, almost entirely dependent on the senses, scent, the fine-grained texture of a man's skin, the smooth play of muscles...

A pulse beat like a trip-hammer in her throat as her body clenched in response to the hidden, subliminal signals.

'Sorry,' he said. 'Did I hurt you?'

Her eyes recoiled from the hard angularity of his features. 'No, not at all,' she said inanely, then added in a little rush. 'I don't really need to have a bath here, I can wait until the helicopter arrives.'

'The chopper isn't going to arrive. It's too close to dusk to risk anything but the most necessary trips now. Your companion is necessary, you are not. Possibly tomorrow, when the floods go down.'

'Perhaps I could get a lift——'

He shook his bronze head. 'Sorry, the road's closed. In Northland, if there's more than four inches of rain a day the hills start to slip away. I estimate that we've had at least six inches since this started last night. And there's more coming. This is a tropical storm, and the latest forecast says it's being chased up by another one from Fiji.'

Oriel said what everyone else had been saying in this unseasonably wet and wild New Zealand summer. 'I'm so *tired* of all this rain. But I can't stay here, I'll be an awful nuisance...' Her voice trailed away under his amused regard, but she finished with an attempt at her normal crispness, 'Unfortunately it sounds as though I have no choice but to accept your hospitality. Thank you.'

'Don't worry, we're geared for guests.'

'Not crippled ones,' she said miserably.

His wide shoulders braced a little as he began to make his way up a shallow flight of stairs. In a more gentle voice he said, 'There's nothing we can do about that now. When did you hurt your foot?'

'I don't know. I didn't look at my watch when it happened.' She swallowed. 'It was nearly nine this morning when the flood came down, and it took me an hour to find David and get him as comfortable as I could.' Her voice wavered, but she didn't mention the nightmare minutes of searching through the floodwaters and the amazing amount of debris brought down by the small creek in the hills, or her growing conviction that David had to be dead. Until at last she had seen him, unconscious and with a broken leg, thrown up by the force of the initial surge on to the bank.

The man carrying her must have understood the panic and dread of those moments, for his arms contracted about her in a comforting hug, and he smiled down into her face, his unusual pewter-coloured eyes compassionate.

'It's all right, you're safe now. Kathy was a nurse before she married and came to live here with her husband. She swears your foot's only wrenched. But it must have been hell walking on it.'

Oriel's mouth stretched wide in a trembling smile. 'It hurt, but I used a stick as a crutch, and when I got to the beach it was easier.'

There was a moment's silence as they both recalled her uneven, staggering progress along the beach, ending in collapse. She had been weeping with exhaustion, but even as he'd raced towards her she had begun to crawl.

He asked brusquely, 'What's your name?'

Colour washed her skin, pale beneath the golden tan she never lost. 'Oriel Radford.'

'I'm Blaize Stephenson.'

'Where is this?' she asked as he manoeuvred her through another door at the landing.

'Pukekaroro, a station on the southern side of the Bay of Islands.'

'Seagull Hill,' she murmured.

'Do you understand Maori?'

'A little. I grew up in Fiji, and although the languages are different the basic structure must be enough alike for me to pick up Maori quite easily when I came to New Zealand.'

He showed a set of strong white teeth in a grin that made him look a little younger than his age—the early thirties, she estimated. 'An unusual upbringing,' he said. His lithe body twisted: for a moment she was pressed hard against him as he negotiated the door into a warmly lit bedroom. Her breath died in her throat as a spark caught fire deep in her body.

Did she imagine it, or did he stiffen slightly? Mortified, she held herself rigid. Without speaking he carried her to another door, also open, where a few strands of scented steam revealed the presence of a bathroom.

There the housekeeper was waiting, a cheerful young woman of thirty or so with red hair and the freckles that went with it, and an air of unquenchable competence. 'Blaize, if you put——'

'Oriel Radford,' he told her. 'Oriel, this is Kathy Howard.'

'How do you do, Miss Radford? Blaize—yes, that's it, on the chair. Fine, I'll be able to cope from now on.'

Again the sensuous flexion of muscle and sinew as he deposited Oriel carefully, managing it so well that she did not knock her foot. Then he said, 'Let Kathy know if there's anything you want, Miss Radford. I'll see you later.'

With him gone the room seemed twice as big. Oriel expelled a breath and smiled cautiously at the housekeeper. 'I hope I'm not being too much of a nuisance,' she said, shyness adding to the natural slight hesitance of her voice.

'Nope—an excitement. We've been shut up here for weeks, it seems, and believe me, we need something to take our minds off the wretched weather! Now, let's get those wet shorts off and you cleaned up a little.'

Half an hour later Oriel was sitting up in bed, a little pale but washed as clean as Kathy's brisk hands could make her, although the face that met her eyes in the hand-mirror was enough to dismay anyone. A long scratch snaked from just below her eye to her chin, blatantly yellow-brown with iodine. Across one of her high cheekbones was a rapidly darkening bruise. To-morrow, she thought gloomily, she was going to have a black eye. Her temple still throbbed, but Kathy's careful examination had convinced her that there was no serious damage, merely another thumping great bruise.

Still, at least the mud had been washed from her hair, although it was drying in a wild aureole of blue-black curls, and the delicious soak in hot water had taken some of the ache from her bones. She looked a real guy, but she was comfortable in spite of the waves of tiredness that washed over her.

Pulling a face at her reflection, Oriel ran long fingers through her hair, trying without much success to control the riotous tangle.

'I'll get you a hairdrier for that,' Kathy said. By now they were on first-name terms. 'It's incredibly thick, isn't it, but fine with it. Glorious!'

Oriel gave her a startled look, but the housekeeper seemed serious enough. Brought up to consider her hair yet another cross to bear, along with her height and her lack of feminine curves and graces, Oriel had grown up listening to her mother complain about the thick mop. Her cousin David had tormented the life out of her by calling her Bushytop, until she grew big enough to enforce her real name. 'It's a nuisance when it's wet,' she murmured. 'Unmanageable.'

'At least it's got a bit of body to it, not like mine.' Kathy found the drier in the bathroom and handed it over before disappearing into the passage. Oriel's hands moved slowly as she dried out the riotous tresses, smoothing them down into some semblance of order. She had just clicked the drier off when the housekeeper reappeared in the doorway carrying a tray with a mug of soup and some crisp toast.

'I'll be back in ten minutes,' she said as she left again. 'See that you've got it all inside you by then.'

Oriel suddenly realised that the ache in her stomach was hunger. Almost greedily she swallowed the soup, which was thin and tasty, finally putting the mug down with a slow, replete smile as she lay back on the pillow, wryly admiring the pale green cotton pyjamas Kathy had found. They fitted around the most important parts, but the legs came halfway up her calves. One of the penalties of being almost six feet tall, she thought whimsically.

In her more self-pitying moments she couldn't decide which physical characteristic had caused her more despair, her height or the fact that, tall as she was, she had narrow hips and almost no bust. An early developer, she had spent years of her life suffering the taunts and teasing that came with being the tallest in the class.

Since then she had grown into the long legs and arms and fought for a hard-won sophistication, but sometimes in moments of stress, such as now, her self-control leached away and she was miserably aware of just how thin a veneer it was. Beneath it, she was still the awkward, shy child who had watched with wondering eyes as her small, exquisite mother charmed everyone in sight.

Some change in the atmosphere, some electricity, lifted her heavy lids. Her heart gave an odd little jump as she focused on Blaize Stephenson, who was almost filling the doorway, bronze hair gleaming with copper highlights as his eyes searched her face. Through lashes that trembled she watched him warily as he came across the room, moving with that loose-limbed grace—a predator's stride, she thought fancifully.

'How are you feeling now?' he asked.

'Much better, thank you.'

He stopped by the big double bed. Oriel immediately felt exposed, the lines of her long legs and body revealed only too clearly by the sheet and thin blanket that was all she had over her. Ignoring twinges of pain, she sat up, curling her bare arms around her knees.

There was a note of irony in the decisive voice as he said, 'I've just been talking to Civil Defence. They got your companion out, and he's all right. You did exactly the right things—splinted his leg and protected him from the weather. He's showing no signs of exposure. The leg is definitely broken, so he's in considerable pain, but he'll come to no permanent damage.'

Sighing, she leaned her head on to her arms, her lashes fluttering down. 'Thank God,' she whispered, relief and weakness releasing the tears she had held back since those first frightening moments of the flood.

The side of the bed depressed. Firmly he brought her across to lie against his shoulder. She hiccupped and tried to pull away, but he held her there, and she succumbed to the age-old masculine comfort, sobbing into the hard warmth.

Humiliated by her weakness, she took a few minutes to regain control. She had almost succeeded in forcing back her tears, ducking her head to hide from those strange silver eyes, but his hand on her chin was irresistible. As gently as though she were a loved child he touched her quivering mouth with a lean forefinger. The tears stopped, making her eyes huge, the blue blurred and slumberous. Again that needle of sensation, hot and frightening, seared through her. Her lashes flicked against the suddenly tender skin of her cheeks.

'All the oracles say that that should have done you the world of good,' he said drily, 'but I must say it rips my heart out to listen to you. Kathy says you're still in shock, so I suppose I'll have to bear with them. She also says there are no bones broken, no great damage done. Now, I want to know exactly what happened.'

She bit her lip, and he resumed gently, but with an inflexible note in the deep tones, 'Tell me, Oriel. I think it will probably be good for you.'

Whether or not, he had been kind when she'd needed it; he deserved to have his very natural curiosity satisfied. She blew her nose on the linen handkerchief he had given her and sat up, banishing the tremor in her voice with stubborn determination. 'I've never seen anything like it—one minute it was in flood, but nothing dramatic, and the next a wall of water and logs and stones came hurtling down the gully. It was terrifying! Dave was in the tent——' Her soft mouth tightened.

'And you were where?'

'I'd just scrambled up the bank to get a better look at it. I was worried. I wanted to see how high the creek had risen, because I thought we were too close. But David wouldn't——' She had wanted to pitch the tent higher up the hill, but David had insisted on setting up camp on a level patch of ground closer to the creek, right in the path of the flood. Still, family loyalty kept her silent.

'It sounded like a train coming at first, and then—a roar like something out of hell. The tent was washed away, and Dave with it, but he was lucky. Somehow the currents tossed him high on the bank out of reach of the rest of the flood, so he didn't drown, but he was hit on the head. I didn't know how badly hurt he was, but he was unconscious for what seemed ages.' She couldn't speak about the appalling minutes when she had searched for her cousin, convinced that he must have been killed.

'So you set out to get help, and you succeeded, in spite of hurting yourself quite badly. I think you should try to get some rest now,' Blaize said quietly, in a voice she found infinitely comforting. 'You're exhausted, and no wonder, after struggling damn near ten miles through the hills. Don't worry about anything, Oriel. You're safe, and everything's under control.'

He was a man you instinctively trusted, with a voice that would make you believe anything, she decided as she watched him go through the door. Which made his promise that she was safe rather a mockery. She doubted very much whether any woman had felt *safe* with Blaize Stephenson since he'd reached puberty.

Perhaps that quick, instinctive trustworthiness had something to do with his size, although such a big man could be threatening—and in some ways he was. Rather uneasily she recalled the moment when her body had responded with a wild *frisson* to his nearness. But he exuded a rock-solid dependability that demanded confidence. He was, of course, totally assured.

It was a quality Oriel envied. The only time she ever felt confident and secure was in front of her class of eight-year-olds. But then, in spite of a nose that had been broken some time ago, Blaize was also very good-looking in a rugged way, which would help. Her roving, slightly dazed mind selected the word Viking. Size again, of course; the Vikings were all huge. And he was fair, with that bronze hair highlighted in glowing amber and copper, and the piercing grey eyes. Tanned skin, though, she thought dreamily, staring down at the golden length of her arms against the white sheets.

And reminiscent of those long-ago sea rovers was the fact that there was something untamed about Blaize Stephenson, a compelling hint of danger that set her instincts jangling.

Which should have sat uneasily with the fact that in spite of his size and the casual clothes he wore with such an air, he emitted a kind of moneyed worldliness she had never encountered before. Of course, at twenty-three Oriel had grown past the stage of being intimidated by rich sophisticates, but somehow it was difficult to convince herself.

Actually the whole set-up was out of place. All through that nightmare trek through the hills she had been making for Pukekaroro, but she had expected it to be like every other large farm she had tramped over. But even as he had carried her across the lawn she had realised that this was like no other homestead she had ever seen.

It was the interior that had really astonished her. Exhausted as she was, a keen sense of beauty had made sure that the house impinged on her consciousness. And inside this house was beauty, simple although far from inexpensive, collected by someone who had a connoisseur's eye and a love of lovely things. Yet the furniture and the objects with which it was decorated did not look stiff and obvious, and for all its loveliness it was definitely a beach house, one where sandy swimmers and children were welcome.

A slight noise at the door lifted her heavy lashes, but it was Kathy, bearing a tray with more food.

Her appetite having fled, Oriel opened her mouth, but before she could object the older woman ordered briskly, 'Eat as much as you can, even if you don't feel like it. You've had an exhausting time and your body needs replenishment.'

Of course she was right. Obediently Oriel ate almost all of the roast chicken and tiny new potatoes and beans, even peeling a fresh peach with a sigh of pleasure. The tangy juice was still sweet in her mouth as she leaned over and placed the tray on the table beside the bed.

Like the rest of the house, her bedroom was beautiful. Buff and cream batik cotton glowed from the windows and the bedspread; in keeping, the bedhead was cane and the pale apricot tiles of the floor were covered in part by a splendid modern rug. A rimu ceiling soared above the room, emphasising the wall of windows. On one wall hung a splendid painting, vivid yet sparely executed, electrifying in its uncompromising evocation of the harsh northern landscape.

Beautiful, but definitely not the sort of bedroom you'd expect to find on a farm, however large and prosperous.

The rain had eased into drizzle, and the wind had died completely, leaving behind a heavy, humid atmosphere that was sticky and unpleasant. Oriel pushed the blankets down past her feet. By hitching herself up a little higher on the pillows she could just see a drenched garden that was still colourful in spite of the wind-drifts of broken petals on the lawn, sad reminders of the wind's ferocity. Through a screen she caught a glimpse of water; frowning, she tried to orientate herself. This room was at the back of the house, so it couldn't be the sea. Besides, it was the wrong colour.

Well, of course, she thought with a slight, disdainful smile. The sea, unpolluted and warm, was at his door, but Blaize Stephenson had a swimming-pool!

It was nearly dark, so it had to be almost nine o'clock, and now that there was relief from the torrential drumming of the rain and screaming of the wind, waves could be heard crashing dramatically on to the beach. Thank God Dave was now safe and marginally comfortable in hospital.

Suddenly drained of her last reserves of strength, she yawned and slipped down on to the pillow. Great surges of weariness rolled over her, and she almost cracked her jaw with another yawn, her tired brain enjoying the simple pleasure and relief of clean sheets and a resilient mattress. As she stretched her long body luxuriously, someone knocked on the door.

'Come in,' she called.

But it was not Kathy who entered, it was Blaize, carrying a water jug and a glass. Oriel's eyes rounded in surprise mixed with alarm. She had dragged the top sheet up to her waist, but even so it revealed too much; the pyjamas were of very thin cotton, and beneath the pale material could be seen her small breasts. With movements that were jerky and clumsy she pulled the sheet up to her chin.

Stupidly, she blushed, and blushed even more when she realised that Blaize was watching her hurried attempt to cover herself with a sardonic smile.

'You look much better,' he said smoothly. 'How's the foot?'

'It's stopped throbbing, thank you.' Her tongue suddenly seemed too big for her mouth; she might be unsophisticated enough to blush, but she wasn't going to give him the satisfaction of realising just how humiliating that impersonal survey had been.

After he had set the jug and glass down on the bedside table he dropped a lurid yellow and pink capsule on to the tray. 'Lemonade. And here's a painkiller, in case your foot starts to hurt during the night. Do you want to read for a while?'

She struggled to lift eyelids made heavy by exhaustion. 'No, thank you. I'd like to go to sleep now.'

He was watching her with a narrowed gaze, a tiny muscle flicking in the arrogant line of his jaw. In spite of her fatigue, in spite of the ten hard miles she had walked that day, something in her responded to that intent, compelling regard. Beneath her heavy eyelids with their drooping corners her eyes went smoky blue. Self-protection lowered her lashes until they rested, quivering, on her cheeks.

In a voice that fairly crackled with authority, he said, 'Right, I'll leave you to it. Goodnight, Oriel.'

''Night.'

The central light died; struggling up on to an elbow, she switched off the lamp, then sank into the oblivion of sleep.

Sun across her eyelids dazzled her into wakening, just as Kathy came in and with her a savoury smell of bacon. Oriel yawned and stretched and wriggled her foot, grimacing a little at the resultant pain, then sat up.

'It's a beautiful morning, and it looks as though the next cyclone has decided to miss us after all. How are you?' the older woman asked cheerfully, setting a tray down on the table. 'Foot still hurting?'

'A little, thank you.' Oriel gave her wide, slightly diffident smile.

'I'll help you into the bathroom and we'll have a look at it.'

Once there Oriel stared horrified at her reflection in the mirror. Oh, the cut on her face was healing, but the bruise on her cheek now encompassed her eye and she looked as though she had gone three rounds with a heavyweight. Just, she thought grimly, like something no self-respecting cat would dream of dragging in!

Shrugging, she washed herself and cleaned her teeth, before wrenching the brush and comb through her hair. In spite of the swollen and bruised state of her foot, she insisted on seeing if she could bear any weight on it, but when she went pale at the pain Kathy bullied her back into bed. There she ate her breakfast, enjoying the home-made muesli and fruit even as she wondered morosely just how long she was going to be imprisoned in Blaize Stephenson's house.

Not long, if the weather was any indication. The heavy easterly swell stirred up by the cyclone still crashed on to the shore, but somehow the sun's warmth robbed the sound of any threat. Oriel's spirits rose, and a smile curved her wide, soft mouth.

How was Dave this morning? Furious, of course, but he was always furious when something spoiled his plans. No doubt he would blame her for it. Oriel frowned, then shrugged. She no longer lived in fear of Dave's frowns, or rather, the family's reactions to them. He had always been the golden boy, the only grandson, the son her mother had wanted, instead of the daughter who was so different from them all.

The adulation hadn't been good for his character. He was so damned difficult, refusing to fit in with the rest of the university tramping party. At the first indication of the storm they had decided to go back, but no, Dave wanted to tramp to the lighthouse, and that was what he was going to do! If Oriel hadn't gone with him he would have pressed on alone, and would quite possibly still be lying out in the hills with his broken leg and concussion. She would never have forgiven herself. And neither, she thought with grim humour, would anyone else in the family, even though the predicament was entirely his own fault.

Her Christmas holidays so far had been an unmitigated disaster, ending with the walk through the hills, a strained foot for herself and a broken leg for her cousin. She only hoped it wasn't any sort of omen for the just-born New Year!

The morning passed fairly quickly. Kathy came up to remake the bed and take away the breakfast tray, and left her with a pile of magazines. Some were fashion glossies, some very house and garden, and Oriel was staring thunderstruck at a room in a house in California, furnished entirely in black leather, when there was another knock on the door.

This time it was Blaize. He smiled at her with lazy appreciation, and she spontaneously showed him the pages. 'Isn't it awful?'

'A troglodyte's paradise,' he said, his eyes amused.

She grinned. 'A cave-dweller? Yes, but why not go and live in a cave, instead of ruining a perfectly good room?'

'You think it's ruined, and so do I, but clearly we're in a minority. Otherwise it wouldn't be in this magazine for *hoi polloi* to admire and copy.'

She chuckled. 'In vinyl?'

'The mind boggles. You look a lot better this morning.'

The mischief in her eyes faded quickly. 'I feel a lot better too, thanks to everyone's kindness. Mr Stephenson, have you heard how David is today?'

Nodding, he pulled up a chair to sit down beside the bed. Even sitting he seemed huge. 'He had a good night. Unfortunately, the X-rays showed a compound fracture, so they decided to take him to Whangarei and reset the leg, and that's where he is now.'

'Do his parents know?'

'Yes, the hospital contacted them last night, and they're driving up from Auckland today. From what the almoner at the hospital said, they seemed determined to arrange his transfer to a hospital closer to home. I believe your mother is on holiday in Australia?'

'Yes.'

He leaned back. 'As there's no real need for her to come back I didn't try to get in touch with her. Is that all right?'

Stifling the suspicion that the question was a mere formality, she didn't tell him that her mother would not be pleased to have her holiday interrupted. Although she would like Blaize—her mother had a connoisseur's eye for men. 'That's perfectly all right,' she said fervently.

He lifted a brow at her in a way she had only ever read about before. It was devastating, conveying a mild surprise and irony at the same time.

'Kathy tells me you can't put any weight on your foot yet. If you feel up to it, I'll take you downstairs,' he drawled.

She gave a quick, involuntary glance downwards at the thin pyjama top. Unbidden colour flaked across her cheekbones. 'I haven't got any clothes to wear,' she said.

'I'm afraid you'll have to use what Kathy can supply,' he said calmly. 'There was no sign of your pack or anything else when I rode up this morning.'

There was nothing of any great worth in her pack, just very basic clothes, shorts, T-shirts and underwear, as well as toiletries she no longer needed. The elegant bathroom next door had soap and toothbrushes and shampoo, creams and lotions and gels, enough for the most fastidious of women.

But she couldn't spend a week or so sitting around this house in borrowed pyjamas. Her thin black brows drew together.

'Don't worry,' he said comfortingly. 'We'll cope.'

She didn't want him to cope. It seemed as though her hard-won independence was being leached away by this dominating, altogether too autocratic man. She didn't want to be carried downstairs in Blaize Stephenson's arms, she didn't want him to look at her as though she were something unusual and more than a little odd, but while she was making up her mind to tell him she'd rather stay in her room he got to his feet with the unforced grace that was so unnerving in such a big man and unhooked a white towelling bathrobe from behind the bathroom door, proffering it on a lean index finger.

'Put it on,' he said, smiling down at her. 'You must be bored out of your mind up here.'

It was no request. In spite of the amusement, he was giving her a direct order. She looked up, met eyes as remote as splinters of crystal, and the defiance that had tasted so good a moment ago flickered and died.

As he walked across to open the door she hauled the robe around her, stuffing her arms into the sleeves and dragging the belt around her narrow waist so that she was covered when he turned.

He lifted her with smooth control, great muscles flowing fluidly as he eased her through the doorway so that her foot was protected from any contact with the walls. As he carried her without effort down the stairs, she realised with a strange inward tremor that he managed to make her feel both weak and small. Not easy to do, she thought with a desperate attempt at her normal pragmatic humour, but of course it was just that he was so big!

She was so busy trying to banish the unusual sensation that she missed her arrival in a room looking out across a lawn, with a view of the sea, now blue and brilliant, through the great branches of the guardian pohutukawa trees.

It was a conservatory with a glass roof; beneath it, protecting the room from the ferocity of the summer sun, were canvas blinds and a creeper that twined luxuriantly across the beams. The floor was made of the same apricot tiles as those in her bedroom; there were palms and plants in pots, and wicker chairs around a circular glass table, and wicker sofas with plump cushions of an artfully faded green and white material. Bifold glass doors were pushed back as far as they could go, letting in the breeze off the sea, fragrant with the scents of this summer coast.

Oriel looked around, concentrating on the scenery— anything to take her mind off the fact that her heart was thumping with unnatural loudness. Outside was a garden, more battered than the one through her window, with drifts of leaves up against flower borders and a transient pool in a dip in the lawn that gleamed silver-green as the sun drained it.

Blaize put her on to a sofa, then, eyes sardonic as though he recognised her instinctive, mindless awareness of him, lifted her legs and arranged their long golden length on it, his fingers lingering a little on the white bandage around her foot. Mesmerised, she tore her eyes away from their lean darkness against the fragile bones of her ankle.

'Is it sore?' he asked.

'No.' She had to clear her throat to say even that. He filled her vision, looming over her. Her imagination running stupidly riot, she likened his stance to that of a hunter, at last within sight of long-sought prey. 'No, it's not at all painful, providing I don't stand on it.'

'Have you tried?'

'This morning.'

'Well, don't do it again.' Straightening, he moved across to a chair, sat down and stretched his long legs out in front of him. 'The doctor at the hospital said it would probably be safe to hobble around on it tomorrow, but that you must rest it as much as you can. It will be at least a week before you're able to walk on it with any degree of comfort, and probably a fortnight before the swelling goes.'

'A fortnight!'

Her expression of blank dismay made him smile ironically. 'Afraid so. Why the despair?'

'I can't possibly stay here for a fortnight!'

'I'm sorry we've given you such a distaste for our hospitality.'

Oriel flushed scarlet, stammering, 'Oh—oh, no, it isn't that! But I can't impose on you for a fortnight, or even a week! You have been very kind and hospitable...' She hesitated, meeting his opaque eyes with determination before finishing, 'But it's not you who has to do the extra work, is it?'

His autocratic face was impassive as he looked at her. 'I don't believe that Kathy has complained about extra work.'

Mockery always reduced Oriel to speechlessness. An inferiority complex, David's mother had diagnosed years ago, and pitied her because she was so tall and gawky, so lacking in poise, so unlike her mother and aunt who were pretty and dainty and charming.

This time, however, she willed herself to relax, meeting the unkind glint in Blaize's smile with unusual resolution. 'No, she hasn't, but having to look after a temporary cripple must make things harder for her.'

'Your consideration for my housekeeper is very touching,' he said blandly, 'but I doubt if it would be well received by her. She's very efficient, and enjoys a chance to display her skills. As the road is still impassable, and likely to stay that way for a few days, I suggest you reconcile yourself to being my guest for at least that length of time.'

She chewed on the inside of her cheek, her shoulders held stiffly as she stared down at her hands. From the corners of her eyes she saw him lean back in his chair and survey her mutinous face with sardonic appreciation.

'Where,' he asked smoothly, 'will you go when you leave here?'

'Home, of course.'

'And home is where?'

'Well, my mother's flat in Auckland.' She actually boarded at the hostel near the school in a small country district in the Waikato, but it was closed over the holidays. Her mother's flat was the closest place to a home for her now.

In a rather more gentle tone he said, 'But your mother is in Australia. When is she coming back?'

'What does it matter when she's coming back? I don't see that it's any of your business——'

He interrupted the angry words with crisp authority. 'On the contrary. If she's coming back to look after you I'll have you conveyed to Auckland, but I'm not sending you back to an empty flat until you're able to look after yourself.'

'Why?' she asked baldly.

He lifted a black brow. 'Even my enemies stop short of accusing me of cruelty to children.'

Antagonism at the mocking indulgence in his voice joined with the familiar feeling of uselessness to form an explosive combination. However, over the years she had learned to control her temper. 'I am not a child,' she said tightly.

He looked bored. 'Then let's say that I couldn't reconcile it with my conscience if I sent you crippled out into the world. When is your mother coming back?'

She had had enough of this. 'I don't really need you to organise my life,' she said in a stifled voice, low but openly hostile. 'I'm grateful for your hospitality, but after the road is opened I'll make my own arrangements, thank you.'

Something flickered in the depths of his eyes, turning cool pewter to molten silver, but his smile was a masterpiece of aloof, uninvolved irony. However, he made no reply to her rude statement, and she felt relief seep sweetly through her tense body.

The quick upward glance she cast at him through the tangled curls of her lashes—her only claim to beauty, as her mother had told all and sundry since her childhood—took in the stark lines of his face. Hard, radiating a tough arrogance, he should have terrified the life out of her, but it was strangely exhilarating to cross swords with him.

'You'll have company shortly,' he said calmly. 'My nephew and niece are arriving within a few days. They've been spending Christmas with their father's parents in Wellington. Simon is fourteen—a nice kid. Sarah is almost seven. They'll be spending the rest of the holidays here.'

'How nice,' she said inadequately.

He gave a wry smile. 'Yes. Unfortunately Sarah was badly affected by her parents' death a few months ago.'

Oriel's tender heart was wrung. She could remember what it was like to lose a beloved parent, and how long it had taken her to stop listening for the footsteps of her father. 'It's one of the most traumatic things that can happen to a child,' she said softly. 'Unfortunately, only time has the cure.'

He looked across at her. 'Your father?'

'Yes.'

'What happened?'

It still hurt, but she said in an even voice, 'He loved skin-diving, and one day he didn't come back.'

'How old were you?'

'Eight.'

'And how long was it before time worked its magic for you?'

'Sometimes,' she said quietly, 'I think it never did. But it was a year before I could say his name without crying, and two or three before I could think of him with a smile.' Her smile was bitter-sweet. 'My mother said——' The words died. She saw him watching her and shrugged. 'My mother felt that I grieved excessively,' she finished wryly. 'She was probably right.'

'Either that, or you have a great capacity for emotion.'

Her shoulders moved again, but it was more of a wriggle than a shrug. She was not in the habit of baring her soul to anyone, let alone a man she had just met and with whom she shared nothing beyond their common humanity.

'No?' he said, his eyes narrowed. 'Well, we'll see how you get on with Sarah. I'd be interested in your professional opinion of her. You did say you were a teacher, didn't you?'

'I'm a teacher, yes,' she returned, 'not a psychologist.'

'Oh, I'm sure you underestimate yourself.' His voice was smooth, and she felt a sudden urge to shout at him, to stamp and swear and shock him out of that smooth mask of sophistication that he wore like an armour.

Horrified by such uncharacteristic fervour, she tamped her runaway emotions down, but he was watching her with a gleam of something like amusement, and that hard, sensual mouth was curled very slightly at the corners. She withdrew, retiring behind the barricades she had constructed so long ago that she was scarcely aware of their existence any more.

CHAPTER TWO

BLAIZE was kind for the rest of the day, talking to Oriel as though she were a valued guest, leaving her when she got tired, and generally being a courteous if somewhat remote host, and when he carried her up to bed again after dinner it was with the impersonal strength of a favourite uncle.

Surprisingly, she was exhausted, although it was barely after nine and the sun had only just gone down behind a pall of scarlet and gold that augured well for the following day. She went to sleep almost immediately, her head sliding sideways on the pillow, the book she was reading slipping from her slender hands on to the coverlet.

It was an old nightmare that disturbed her, but familiarity had never dulled the edge of terror. She was being chased by something, an unknowable, horrible thing that was catching her. She was running through water, cold, thick black water that dragged at her ankles, impeding her with slimy ropes and strings. Petrified, her heart beating like a painful drum in her ears, her chest straining as she tried to drag in agonising breaths of air, she couldn't move, but a little way off was the land, sunlit and smooth, and if she could get there she would be safe from the horror. She could hear it breathe behind her, smell its foul stench. Closer—closer...

'Wake up, Oriel! It's only a dream! Come on, wake up.'

Abrupt, imperative, the curt command penetrated the chaos of terror. Gasping, her hands stretched out im-

ploringly, she fought her way through to wakefulness.
Someone was shaking her shoulder, the fingers strong
and firm.

The sobs died in her throat as she opened her eyes to
meet the silver flames of Blaize's eyes. Staring mutely,
she became shamingly conscious of the way she was
clutching his robe as though he were her only hope of
salvation. She jerked away to huddle back against the
headboard, desperately striving to control the shudders
that racked her body. Slowly the panic faded and the
colour washed back into her eyes, making them darker,
smokily dazed.

Ignoring her silent resistance, he sat on the bed and
with a careless strength propped her against his shoulder,
her cheek pillowed in the dark blue material of his robe.
The sleek muscles of his torso were hard and warm; she
found herself relaxing, comforted by a sense of security
she had never experienced before.

'Better?' he asked after a moment, his hand stroking
rhythmically up and down her back.

She stiffened, but he continued stroking, the smooth
movement of his palm soothing, completely without
threat. Hiccupping, she nodded.

His chest lifted as he laughed. 'Your hair tickles. No,
don't wriggle away, think of me as your favourite uncle.
Do you often have nightmares?'

'I haven't had one for ages. Was I screaming?'

After a moment's pause he said quietly, 'You were
calling for your father.'

She bit her lip and drew a deep breath, but before she
could say anything he went on, 'I'm sorry if anything I
said today caused this. I had no idea I'd be turning loose
such—such raw memories.'

'You didn't,' she whispered. 'I don't know why I had
it tonight. I'm not neurotically fixated on my father's
death, or anything. I came to terms with it years ago.'

'Perhaps telling you about Sarah and Simon brought it all back.'

It seemed likely, so she nodded, her weighted lashes falling as the overdose of emotion and the gentle movements of his hand on her back worked their inevitable magic.

Still holding her against him, he leaned back against the pillows. With the sound of his heart thumping quietly in her ears, the scent of his male presence in her nostrils, she allowed this comfort, freely and generously given, to lull her into a peaceful, dreamy calmness.

'All right?'

At her murmured assent he eased her down on to the pillows and got up. Bereft, she still managed a drowsy smile. He chuckled, and said, 'You look like a small squirrel.'

His voice came closer; she opened her eyes just as his mouth touched hers, warm and firm. Her heart almost stopped. An explosion of the senses shattered her peace, a shock of awareness so powerful it branded every cell in her body.

When he jerked upright her dilated eyes saw his lips move in what must have been some sort of oath, and watched astonishment and shock empty his face of all expression but sheer, uncompromising control. There was no recognition in his regard—it was almost as though she were not there and he was seeing someone else in her place. His mouth clenched into a straight, hard line, his narrowed gaze was bleak and cold as he stared right through her, every angle of his face emphasised into a harsh menace in the warm glow of the light.

At last he said on a curiously level note, 'Do you think you might be able to sleep now?'

'Yes. Thank you.' She felt slightly sick, her body aching with a febrile, unknown excitement. 'You've been very kind. I'm sorry I disturbed you.'

His eyes narrowed as he searched her face. 'So am I,' he said through lips that barely moved. 'Goodnight.'

For a long time after he turned the light out she lay huddled in the bed. The air was damp and hot, sticky with the scents of the night, and she was unable to sleep until the first pale seepage of dawn came into her room.

In the morning the incident seemed as much a dream as the nightmare, and every bit as upsetting.

While she ate her breakfast in the security of her bedroom she decided that the sooner she was gone from this place and Blaize Stephenson the better. Last night she had come close to making a great fool of herself, and she wasn't going to suffer the humiliation of developing a king-size crush on the man if she could possibly avoid it.

The promise of the sunset had been fulfilled. As she limped gingerly across the room she admired the fresh, bright greens of the countryside spread out above the garden, the bold contours of the hills heightened by the golden wash of summer. In the garden flowers held up their colourful faces, uncaring that a few days before the same sky had hurled tempest and ruin at them.

Cattle moved across a hillside, big beasts, pale gold against the startling freshness of the grass, harassed by a black and white dog, followed by a man on a horse. Blaize? No, this was a smaller man, and when he told the dog explicitly where it had gone wrong, Oriel recognised a broad New Zealand accent. Unlike Blaize, who sounded English but spoke with New Zealand speech patterns, which meant, she decided, either English parents and a New Zealand upbringing, or very upperclass New Zealand parents.

Her reluctant mind returned to those sweet yet frightening moments the night before when he had held her gently, and the strange pagan aftermath. If she closed her eyes...

With a very great effort she forced her eyes open. Blaize was the sort of man adolescent fantasies were made of, tall and broad and strong, handsome with that hint of untamed depths that had such an irresistible appeal to most women. But not to Oriel Radford. At twenty-three, she told herself briskly, she was well past daydreaming. It led to pain and humiliation, all the things she could most emphatically do without!

When Kathy came up to collect her tray Oriel was seated in the chair by the window, trying to untangle the knots in her hair.

'How's the foot today?' asked Kathy.

She smiled. 'Much better. If I limp carefully and hang on to the furniture I can get around quite easily. It doesn't even hurt much.'

'Just as well I got your clothes washed and dry, then,' the older woman said. 'I'll bring them up.'

Half an hour later, with Kathy in close attendance, Oriel made her way down the stairs, frowning a little in concentration as she negotiated them. She had already miscalculated once, and the ensuing pain convinced her that she needed to go slowly and very carefully.

Blaize's voice, with a reverberation like the crack of a whip, made her flinch and lose her balance, clutch vainly at the banister and sit down abruptly.

'What the hell are you doing?'

She said spiritedly, 'I was coming down the stairs until you scared me!'

There was an odd silence, during which she heard the older woman draw in a sharp breath, before he said crisply, 'I'm sorry. Should you be putting any weight on that foot?'

She explained again that it didn't hurt provided she was careful. He wasn't entirely satisfied and demanded a demonstration, watching her keenly as she carefully limped towards him. Self-consciousness made her falter and pain shot through her foot. She thought she hid the wince well, but his frown deepened and she braced herself for instructions to stay put all day.

However, almost as though he begrudged the words, he agreed finally, 'Very well, then, although if you walk much on it the extra strain will make your other hip painful. Come into the sun-room and sit down. A liner's going past on the way out from Opua, if you're interested.'

He was very elegant in a pair of dark blue trousers with a pale blue shirt on top, his glowing head catching the sunlight in a bedazzlement of light and colour.

'Here.' He handed her a pair of binoculars. 'Take a closer look.'

'Oh, she's lovely,' she breathed, unaware of the naked longing in her voice, or the speculative glance he cast her.

'Isn't she? She came in yesterday morning and is heading for Suva now.'

'Fiji,' she sighed, her eyes steady on the white hull and graceful lines.

'Yes. Whereabouts did you live when you were there?'

She smiled sadly. 'I was born in Suva, but home was one of the Yasawa Islands. My father owned a tourist complex there. When he died we came back to be closer to my mother's family in New Zealand. Her parents are still alive, and she's close to a sister in Auckland. Daddy was English, but he would never have gone back. He adored Fiji and the tropics.'

'Do you remember much about it?'

Carefully she removed the binoculars and put them on the table. A subtle note of wistfulness deepened her voice as she replied, 'I remember the sun, and the sea, and trying to climb coconut palms with other children. And church—the Fijians sang so beautifully. My mother says I ran wild.' Her smile was spiced by a momentary gleam of mischief. 'I remember a full set of Fijian swear words that come in useful now and then.'

Laughing, he held out his hand for the binoculars. As she passed them over she thought bemusedly that he had beautiful hands, lean and tanned, with long fingers and short, blunt nails. A scandalous piece of imagery made her blush scarlet and turn her head swiftly away. She was not going to allow her stupid imagination to embarrass her by visualising just how those hands would look against her skin.

A surreptitious glance revealed that he had not noticed—he was still watching the liner as she moved out towards the open sea. Against the light from the window his profile was a bold slash, all straight lines and angles apart from the curves of his mouth. It was aggressive yet profoundly attractive: wide forehead and sweeping cheekbones, a thin-bridged nose with its intriguing disjunction, an autocratic line of jaw and chin; the surprisingly sensual shaping of his mouth should have contrasted, perhaps even watered down the effect of inborn strength and authority, but it didn't.

She thought, with a tiny *frisson* of shock at her own daring, that although Blaize was definitely a sensuous man his passions would always be controlled by his will. The strong sweep of jaw and the hint of disciplined toughness in his mouth revealed more than the deliberate self-sufficiency of his usual expression.

He turned, and she hastily lowered her eyes, aware that in her cheeks there was enough wildfire colour to give him some indication of the way her thoughts had been heading.

'Did you get back to sleep after your dream last night?'

'Oh, yes,' she said brightly and not quite untruthfully. It wasn't the dream that had kept her awake.

'Good.' He changed the subject, saying, 'I have to go into Russell this afternoon, and so does Kathy. Will you be all right?'

'Yes, of course I will.'

He gave her a somewhat cynical smile. 'Just be careful. If you wrench that foot again you may well be wearing sandals for several months.'

'If it will make you happier, I'll stay on my bed all afternoon,' she said shortly. She was not accustomed to such solicitude; her mother had never 'fussed', as she called it, and Oriel had been on her own too long to enjoy it now.

His eyebrow lifted. She saw his recollection of the night before in his expression, and embarrassment at her gaucheness heated her cheeks. But all he said, and that very urbanely, was, 'A good idea.'

It was with the sound of that enigmatic remark in her ears that she stripped off her shorts and T-shirt and lay on the bed in her underwear, first making sure the big launch had disappeared behind the headland. To her surprise she slept for several hours, waking stiff and lethargic and depressed. She lay listening, but apart from the sound of the waves there was nothing. They must still be in Russell.

The house seemed very empty while he—while they, she corrected with a frown, were away. With a sigh she made her way across to the desk and sat down to write to her mother.

It was difficult; the time was long gone when they had much to say to each other. Jo Radford was a small, dainty blonde who frequently bewailed the fact that her only child was tall and thin and dark, with none of her delicate beauty. The dissimilarities extended even further than that. Newly widowed and left with barely enough money to keep them, Jo had found a job in a model agency, a situation where her looks and her interests worked for her.

She enjoyed the life immensely, relishing her contacts with the creative and the rich; an occasion in Auckland wasn't really an occasion unless Jo Radford was there, her delicate features exquisitely made up, her dress sense impeccable. Wittily malicious, amusing, always to be relied on, Jo was part of the Auckland 'scene'.

Which was fine. Except that Jo had never been able to resist mourning a daughter who was clumsy and ungainly, totally lacking in wit, and obstinately uninterested in the world her mother had made her own.

But she did, as she was fond of saying, do her best for the child. Oriel had been sent to an exclusive boarding-school where she'd rubbed shoulders with the children of the rich and the famous, she had had all the right lessons—ballet, music, drama, tennis—in the process imperceptibly losing much of the clumsiness that so irritated her mother.

Then there had been a further disappointment when she had opted for that most unfashionable of careers, primary school teaching.

Oriel grimaced. She could still hear her mother's voice as she wailed, 'Why don't you take a commerce degree at university? Really, Oriel, the one thing you do have is brains! Teaching! For heaven's sake, no one who is anyone goes teaching now, it's so—so sexist! Only old-fashioned women who want to get married and have stacks of babies teach!'

But as well as being a disappointment, Oriel was stubborn. She liked children, and she felt that teaching them was a very worthwhile profession, one that would give her satisfaction, one where she was needed. With the quiet determination that her mother stigmatised as obstinacy, she persisted in her ambition. So far, in her second year out from training college, she had not felt a moment's disenchantment with the career she had chosen.

Her gaze fell on the writing paper. Wide mouth pulling in at the corners, she began the letter. Soon she was so deeply immersed in tactfully telling her mother what had happened that she didn't hear the deep throb of the launch as it came into the bay.

It was a knock on the door that interrupted her. 'Come in,' she called, pushing the paper away with a certain amount of shamed relief.

In came Kathy, bearing boxes. 'Clothes,' she said succinctly. At Oriel's bewildered look she dumped them on the bed and explained, 'From Russell. I bought you some skirts and blouses, a few odds and ends and a couple of pairs of jandals.'

'That's very kind of you.' Oriel limped across to the bed. 'I'm afraid you'll have to wait until I can get to the bank before I can pay you.'

'No hurry.' Kathy hesitated, then said offhandedly, 'Actually, Blaize paid for them. He's not going to hassle you for the money, so don't worry about it.'

'I can't——' Oriel stopped, frowning. Every instinct rose in protest, but it would be stupid to object too vigorously to a mere kind-hearted gesture. And she had to have something to wear other than the things she had on! Lamely, she finished, 'Well, of course it's very kind of him. And of you.'

'Oh, he told me to buy whatever you needed.'

'I'll see about paying him later, then.' The words were bitter in her mouth, but she forced them out. 'And I must admit I'll be glad to get out of these grotty old shorts.'

Kathy grinned. 'Yes, they've certainly seen better days, haven't they? I hope I got your size right.'

She had. The clothes fitted perfectly, although the colours were not ones Oriel would have chosen, being bold and glowing, and the styles were too conspicuous. When it had become obvious that Oriel was going to be very close to six feet tall, her mother had decreed that she should dress conservatively, and, as she always did when it came to Jo's areas of expertise, Oriel had agreed wholeheartedly with her.

However, she was not going to spoil Kathy's pleasure in her choices, so she smiled as she pulled out a bright ice-pink skirt, full and flounced, and a singlet top, tie-dyed in white and the same glowing pink, that revealed only too blatantly the unfeminine breadth of her shoulders and the even more unfemininely small breasts, so out of proportion to the rest of her.

'Try them on,' Kathy urged eagerly, and when she had pulled them on, 'Oh, *yes*, I thought they'd suit you. Wait a minute.'

She pulled open the doors of the wardrobes on one wall to reveal full-length mirrors. 'There, take a look,' she invited, beaming.

To Oriel's surprise she didn't look too garish; her height carried off the gypsy flounces in the skirt, and her smooth, tanned shoulders looked good beneath the wide neck. Paradoxically, the clinging bareness of the top showed her breasts in a very kindly light. And surprisingly enough, because it wasn't one she would ever have thought she could wear, the colour suited her too.

'You've got a good eye,' she said, turning to smile at the older woman. 'Thank you for going to so much trouble.'

Kathy grinned. 'No problem. There's some underwear there too, but it seemed wiser just to get T-shirt bras. You're so nice and neat you don't really need to wear one at all, do you?'

Oriel cringed at the thought of going without a bra. T-shirt bras were better than nothing, but they were altogether too—unstructured, she thought with a wry inner smile. For 'structure' read a little tactful padding.

Of course she couldn't tell Kathy that, so she smiled and nodded, and hobbled back to the bed to check out the rest of the clothes. There were several other skirts, all full so that they were easy to pull on, two shirts, and a couple of sun-dresses, one with a small jacket as a cover-up, all in the vivid jewel colours that Kathy clearly liked so much—brilliant blue, bright tropical greens and pinks, and glowing reds.

There were also a couple of muslin sarongs with a fine cotton fringe. 'They're awfully handy for covering up after a swim,' Kathy explained. 'Oh, and some togs too.'

The bathing-suit in thin hot-pink lycra with a black panel down the front would, Oriel knew with a sigh of resignation, emphasise her height and reveal the bony frame of her body only too clearly. Still, all bathing-suits did.

At the bottom was a box, and Oriel's brows shot up as she read the rather famous name on it. Anything from this particular designer was inordinately expensive.

'Blaize said you'd need something to wear at night,' Kathy said casually. 'He does quite a bit of entertaining here, and you'll definitely be here for the end of the holidays "do". You can't wear a sun-frock, however pretty, to that. In some ways it's the social highlight of the season for the district.'

'I can't wear a dress from Decadence, either,' Oriel told her drily. 'My mother works in the fashion industry and I know how much those creations cost. I can't afford one.'

'Well, try it on,' Kathy coaxed. 'I'd love to see you in it. I had great fun picking it out.' She laughed and looked down at her own slightly opulent curves. 'Go on, give me a vicarious thrill! I'll never be able to get into anything from Decadence. They only design for race-horse ladies, all sleek and fine-boned and tall.'

Put like that, how could Oriel refuse? Very carefully she opened the box, drawing a quick breath at the bold stripes in raspberry and white taffeta. It was a skirt, bouffant and reeking of bravado, and to go with it a white lycra and cotton top, long-sleeved, high-necked in front, and with the back scooped out right to the waist.

'No, don't wear a bra,' Kathy said, tactfully turning her head away in case Oriel was shy. 'You don't need one, and it will spoil the line of the top.'

With resignation Oriel stripped off. Taking extreme care, she wriggled into the top and donned the skirt, standing with outward patience and a stirring of secret anticipation while Kathy tied a sash of raspberry silk around her waist. Then slowly she looked at herself in the mirror. Even barefoot she looked wonderful, the vibrant colour suiting her perfectly, the brash material somehow toned down by the elegantly scandalous top to witty chicness.

'Wow,' Kathy breathed. 'You look—stunning!'

Oriel was astounded. Never in her wildest dreams would she have thought of even trying on such an outfit, yet she could see that it did more for her than any of her clothes ever had. Well, naturally, she thought, as she turned to catch a glimpse of a wide expanse of tanned, silky back. Somehow, by some mysterious alchemy, the clever little outfit even made her look sexy!

But as astonishing as the fact that the style looked so good on her was what the colours did. Instead of being faintly sallow her skin glowed like a golden seduction, and her eyes were huge and smokily inviting in a face that seemed suddenly catlike with the slanted line of her eyes and brows, wide, high cheekbones and pointed chin. Even her mouth glowed, pink and soft and a little tremulous.

Clearly, her mother's decree that she dress inconspicuously had been well off the mark. Jo wore her clothes so superbly that it had never occurred to Oriel to question her wisdom, but now, scanning the bright, dashing figure in the glass, she realised that for once her mother had made the wrong fashion statement. In the future, she decided, whirling carefully, she would be a little more adventurous with colours.

'It's gorgeous, but of course I can't keep it,' she said on a sigh. 'Not that it matters, because I'm not going to be here when Blaize has this party. And even if I were, I wouldn't come down.'

Kathy looked surprised. 'Why ever not?'

'Well, I'm not exactly an ordinary guest, am I? More like the Ancient Mariner at the wedding feast. Uninvited.'

'Don't be silly—Blaize isn't a snob.'

Oriel looked stubborn. 'I'm sure he's not, but——'

'Then you're the snob.'

After an astonished moment Oriel gave a lop-sided, deprecating grin. 'You don't pull any punches, do you? I don't think I'm a snob, but you must see what I mean.'

'I think you're too sensitive for your own good. Rest assured, if Blaize didn't want you here he'd have found some way of getting you off the property. He might be the best boss I've ever worked for, but he can be a ruthless swine when he wants to be. You're here, and so he wants you here, for whatever reasons. Which are none of my business,' Kathy said, briskly getting to her feet. 'What *is* my business is getting dinner, and I'd better start on it right away!'

But she stayed long enough to hang the other clothes in the wardrobe and put the underclothes and two short nightgowns away, while Oriel struggled gingerly out of the Decadence outfit. However, when she began to repack the skirt and blouse and sash in the layers of tissue paper, Kathy came over and whipped them away.

'They'll be better hanging up,' she said firmly before picking up the boxes and leaving the room.

Oriel sat down rather limply. 'Damned foot,' she said angrily, scowling at its thin, bandaged length. It kept her immobile and slow, and it was infuriating.

Still, she was relieved to have the clothes. At least she no longer had to struggle into faded, tight, definitely seen-better-days denim shorts. After pulling on the pink skirt and its matching top, she carefully made her way down the stairs to the sun-room, her letter to her mother in her hand. Perhaps she would have better luck finishing it there.

But when Blaize came in a few minutes later, tanned and virile in light trousers and a fine Italian cotton shirt, she was staring out at the intriguing roof of what appeared to be a gazebo, or summer-house, seen through a screen of gardenia bushes.

'What's this I hear about your refusing to wear the clothes Kathy chose?' he asked without preamble, his voice forbiddingly curt.

Her mouth firmed as she made an abrupt gesture at the flounce of bright material across her knees. 'You can see that I'm wearing them.'

'But you don't intend to keep all of them.'

Shrugging, she allowed her lashes to cover the mutinous blue of her eyes. 'I don't need and can't afford an outfit by Decadence. I'm sure the shop will take it back.'

'You don't know how much it cost.'

She snorted. 'I know it costs too much for me to be able to afford.'

He sat down opposite her, meeting her gaze with a cool intimidation that made her draw back behind the barricades, her flash of defiance temporarily subdued. Instinct had told her that he was a formidable man; now she was seeing it in action. Uncertainly she said, 'Mr Stephenson——'

'Blaize.'

'Blaize, then. I don't need a dress like that. I'm a schoolteacher in a small country town, where the social life is informal, and where I don't——'

'Every small country town has at least one ball every year,' he countered blandly. 'I'm sure the Young Farmers' Club would love to see you in a dress by Decadence.'

She cast him a cold look, something inside flinching at the unkind humour in his face. 'I already have a ball-gown. I don't need another.'

'You'll need it here. I'm having a fairly large party to mark the end of the holidays, and——'

'I won't be here,' she snapped, goaded by his refusal to allow her to get out of the situation with any dignity. 'I'll be back at home. And even if I'm not, I won't come to a party I have no right to attend.'

'It's only a couple of weeks away, so you'll still be here. And you'll come, my girl.' He gave her a lazy, totally determined smile, his voice smoothing into a languorous caress that stroked over her nerves like warm honey. 'I refuse to allow you to lurk in your bedroom like a mad relative in a melodrama.'

She couldn't stop the chuckle that burst through her irritation. He grinned, and the charm was so potent that she could only keep smiling like an idiot.

On a note of indolent amusement he said, 'If the thought of paying for it gives you any pain, let me. I'll be glad——'

'No!'

Ignoring her, he went on, 'Think of it as a belated Christmas present. Or an early birthday present.'

Gritting her teeth, she began formally, 'Mr——'

'Blaize.'

'Blaize, one thing my mother made sure I understood was that a man who buys presents often thinks he has the right to buy other things, some of which I might not feel like selling. It took me about five years to work out what the hell she meant, but I finally got there, and I am not going to let you pay for my clothes.'

He lifted that infuriating brow. 'I don't see how you're going to stop me,' he said with smooth effrontery. 'However, if it will set your mind at rest, I'm not in the habit of demanding that anyone pay their debts by sleeping with me.'

Scarlet, she spluttered, but rallied quickly. 'I won't wear them.'

He was still smiling, but as he leaned forward all the amusement vanished from his expression and he was very forbidding indeed. 'If you don't, Oriel, I shall personally dress and undress you myself. I don't want to hear any more mealy-mouthed middle-class posturings from you. You'll wear what's in the wardrobe if I have to put the horrors you've been getting around in into the shredder. And you will smile and look as though you are enjoying them, because Kathy went to a great deal of trouble to choose them for you, and I will not have her upset. If it helps to sweeten the pill, I'm rich enough for those few outfits to make no dent in my petty cash, and I like to see attractive women around me, not waifs apparently dressed by the nearest charity shop. Allow me my idiosyncrasies, especially as I'm prepared to pay for them.'

Oriel was a teacher. Always comparatively placid, she had learned how to control her temper. The children in her class knew that it took a lot to make Miss Radford mad. But instead of being cowed by this blighting summary of her charms and behaviour she felt temper swish through her from her stomach to the top of her head. Even her legs trembled.

Her hands clenched by her sides as she thrust her chin out and said in the molten tones of incandescent rage, 'You are an arrogant, authoritarian bastard, and I am not going to come to your damned party or wear your damned clothes if I have to swim to Russell to get away from you.'

'You had better,' he retorted through his teeth, his eyes silver as swords at dawn, 'get there very quickly, because if I come after you you'll be sorry you tried. You damned well won't be sitting down for a week!'

Shocked, her eyes great wells of stormy outrage, she jumped to her feet, only to bite back a groan and collapse into the chair.

'You stupid little fool!' He was beside her before she had time to regain control, his lean, strong fingers oddly gentle as they lifted her foot on to a hassock.

'I'll take you in to the doctor,' he said, unwrapping the bandage. 'In spite of Kathy's expertise, I'll feel a lot happier once it's X-rayed.'

Horrified at her bout of temper, appalled at the things she had said, the names she had called him, Oriel watched passively as he examined her foot with a deft gentleness that drained the fury from her in a black flood, leaving her spent and tired. Never in her life had she felt such anger, and for a man who had been unequivocally kind to her, if a little arrogant and highhanded.

Painfully, the words bleak, she said, 'I'm sorry.'

He looked up, his fingers stilling. 'Why?'

'For being so rude.' His eyes were very perceptive, too sharp. Lashes falling, she turned her head away.

'For losing your temper? Why not? I lost mine, and said some unforgivable things.'

His hand was stroking her instep, gently turning the foot, moving the bruised and darkened flesh until she made a small noise. 'I'm almost certain there are no broken bones,' he said absently. 'You've just wrenched it very badly. Nevertheless, you can go in to see the doctor tomorrow, just to reassure me.'

'I don't want——' She stopped, meeting his limpid gaze with something like desperation.

'Wise girl,' he said smoothly, after a second when unspoken words had hummed like high-tension wires. 'I'll get the tourist helicopter to come and pick us up.'

Her features rigid with self-imposed control, she asked, 'Are you always like this?'

'Like what?'

She wasn't fooled by the amused expression on the handsome face. 'Like a bulldozer.'

'Yes. It makes things much easier for me. And ultimately for you too. You see, you don't have to worry whether you're doing the right thing, or about your mother's precepts and homilies, you can just sit back and let me do the deciding for you, secure in the knowledge that there's nothing you can do about it. I always get my own way—it's a habit I've acquired.'

'You're an insufferable egotist,' she said, but without heat. 'And a tease.'

Deftly he rewrapped her foot, ran his finger with exquisite precision up her calf, and watched with a connoisseur's eye as she blushed.

'Men are not teases,' he said, and bent to kiss the side of her mouth before he left her, smiling crookedly.

She leaned back into the chair, feeling as though she had been shot through the heart. His mouth had been warm and firm and gentle, yet once again her body had responded with a lightning clamour at his touch. Wondering if he too felt it, she tried to take her mind off the incredible things she had said and done by picking up a book on New Zealand she found on the table.

It was signed by the author, a man whose name she recognised as one of the best-known travel writers of the decade, famous for his perception and intellect. The book, she recalled, had been enthusiastically received in some quarters, lambasted for its savage dissection of the country in others. He had signed it, addressing it to Blaize, in memory of days spent talking and nights spent enjoying. Enjoying what?

Who, or what, was Blaize Stephenson? A rich man, clearly, a friend of the famous. Famous himself? His name niggled in the back of her mind, but try as she could she didn't recall where she had seen or heard it before.

If he wasn't famous it was because he didn't want to be, she decided, staring at the frontispiece. He had that sort of aura, of authority and power, the calmly arrogant strength of a man who has made his place in the world.

CHAPTER THREE

THE day wore on to an end, the sun moving slowly across the great bowl of the sky. It was very hot; too hot. After another hour spent struggling with the letter to her mother, Oriel limped across to the window to look longingly at the crisp blue of the sea.

Situated as the farm was, halfway out to the southern head of the Bay of Islands, there were far fewer yachts to be seen than at the head of the Bay off Paihia and the Kerikeri inlet, but as she watched two came into view from the open sea. They had probably come up from Auckland to spend the rest of the school holidays here in paradise.

Her father had had a yacht. Memories of long days spent under a burning tropical sun teased her brain, and the strong lines of her father's laughing face as he steered through smiling, frolicking dolphins.

Everything had come to an end when he'd died. Much more vivid was her memory of the cold and rain in Auckland when they had moved back, and her bewilderment at the noise and bustle of the city, her longing for the heat and the undemanding companionship of the children she had known, the indulgence of their parents.

It had been a shock, one she had never really got over, and she had never quite been able to fit into life in New Zealand. Perhaps, she thought with a wry smile, it was one of the reasons for her diffidence.

Which brought back uncomfortably vivid memories of how she had lost that diffidence to shout at Blaize, calling him names and behaving with all the flair and sophistication of a fishwife. Heat stained her skin as she suffered embarrassment all over again. What on earth must he have thought of her?

A long-forgotten but familiar scent floated in on the air; eager to banish her thoughts, she leaned out through the window and looked along the wall. A few feet away were the round, smooth branches of a frangipani bearing great bunches of creamy pink flowers, the sight of them immediately flooding her with another wave of nostalgia. Just such a bush, only taller and more lush, had grown by the gate to their house in Fiji. Perhaps her subconscious had recognised the scent, which would explain the bout of self-pity a few minutes ago.

Moving cautiously, she made her way along the path of crushed shell, stopping to drink in the heavenly, evocative fragrance, her eyes misty with memories. This had to be about as far south of the Equator as frangipani would grow, and it probably wouldn't thrive anywhere but close to the sea. Smiling, she picked one of the flowers and tucked it behind her ear.

'Appropriate.'

Blaize's drawl spun her around, but she stayed upright. Rather breathlessly she said, 'I hope it's not forbidden to pick anything.'

He was standing with his back to the sun so she couldn't see the expression on his face too clearly, but his voice was level as he said, 'I can think of few more suitable places to see a flower. The colour and texture complement your skin and hair perfectly. Feel free to pick anything you like.'

'Thank you,' she said, struggling to hide her surprise. The underlying note of intensity in the words bewildered her, as did his throwaway delivery of them.

'Dinner will be ready in an hour,' he said with a hint of formality. 'Would you like to change?'

She hesitated, then told him a little awkwardly, 'I'd rather eat in my room, if it's all right. My foot seems to have swollen again.'

'Of course.' Before she had time to object he picked her up and carried her carefully up to her bedroom.

After she had thanked him she didn't see him again that night, for which she was heartily thankful. He might not care when women screamed at him with the finesse of a navvy, but she was not accustomed to losing control like that, and the memories made her writhe with shame.

However, when he tapped at her door at nine-thirty the next morning he appeared to have forgotten entirely about the whole humiliating incident, for the smile he gave her warmed her right down to the pit of her stomach.

Forewarned by Kathy, she was ready for the trip to the doctor, and even endured with outward composure the trial of being carried out in Blaize's strong arms to a Range Rover in the gravel court behind the house. No one, she hoped, could have any idea of how relieved she was going to be when she could get around once more, and no longer had to suffer the refined sadism of being held so firmly yet so impersonally against him.

It helped if she bent her eyes and attention on the surroundings, so she gazed around with profound interest as she was transferred to a paddock where the rowdy helicopter stood waiting, its rotors sending sheep fleeing across the hills to a safe distance. On the flat land behind the beach were two other houses, neat behind their hedges. There were farm buildings, and yards, a paddock holding some truly enormous bulls and, beside a gate, a large woolshed. Oriel looked rather longingly at the road that wound from the gate to a valley in the backing hills.

Blaize put her carefully into the narrow seat, helping her with that disturbing gentleness to buckle up. 'OK?' he mouthed, his eyes narrowing as they scanned her face.

Oriel nodded. He lifted a thumb to the pilot. The engines changed pitch and the machine rose gently from the ground. After the initial butterflies Oriel peered eagerly out, her face alive with interest. Flying over the Bay was thrilling, looking down on yachts like small butterflies hovering over water the colour of lapis lazuli. Emphasised by hills startlingly green with grass, stands of forest rose from the calm enclosure of the Bay to high blue ridges.

She enjoyed it immensely, although she did not like arriving at Paihia as the focus of a crowd of tourists, all of whom, it seemed to her, watched with avid speculation as Blaize calmly climbed out, plucked her from the machine and strode across to a waiting car that took her the hundred or so yards to the surgery.

'What's the matter?' he asked.

Oh, he missed nothing, although she had tried to hide behind an impassive front. Still flushed, she hissed at him, 'I hate being a sideshow!'

He grinned. 'Don't be mean. They loved it. Every man was wishing he was the one with such a delectable armful——'

'And every woman wished you were carrying her. So romantic!' she snapped back, and flushed again at his open laughter, the not unkind mockery in the pewter eyes.

All in all she was glad when she was back in the helicopter, although the return trip to the landing pad had been even worse. One of the ferries from Russell had just arrived at the wharf, and the business of being transferred to the chopper was watched with eagerness and more than a few comments, all complimentary and some of them surprisingly frank, by every passenger ambling down the long jetty.

It was no wonder her cheeks were blazing when at last she pulled the seatbelt tight. Blaize was openly laughing.

But at least the doctor had agreed that her foot was just wrenched, with no sprain and no broken bones. Of course, in answer to a query from Blaize, he'd also said that she should keep off it as much as possible until the swelling went down. Blaize had suggested crutches.

'Not really necessary,' the doctor had said, smiling benignly at Oriel. She had not wanted Blaize in the surgery with her, but clearly it had never occurred to the doctor to keep him out, and from the subsequent conversation it had transpired that they were old fishing mates.

'No,' she'd said firmly. 'I can get around easily enough. Would it be possible for me to go back home?'

'Is there anyone to take care of you?' At her headshake the doctor had said matter-of-factly, 'Well, you wouldn't die, but I'm much happier at the thought of you staying with Blaize. Kathy's a good nurse, and it will heal faster if you stay off it as much as possible.'

She couldn't help stealing a glance at Blaize and had met mockery mixed with satisfaction in his smile. It made her suspicious enough to be silent all the way back to Pukekaroro.

Once there she ate a delicious lunch with a host whose deliberate use of charm increased her suspicions, then rested for a couple of hours. She should have slept, for the morning's expedition had proved that she had still not recovered from the demands she had made on her body the day of the flood, but she couldn't get that open male satisfaction out of her brain.

It was stupid, for what would Blaize Stephenson want from her? The first answer, her body, was hastily dismissed. Men like him, handsome as sin, rich and worldly, did not want small-town teachers as lovers, however temporary. She had seen photographs of the women they made love to. Beautiful, superbly dressed, with sophistication coming out of their wonderfully manicured fingertips.

Profoundly irritated by her thoughts, she told herself that of course he didn't want anything from her! He was merely the sort of autocrat who liked to be right all the time, and so was pleased that the doctor's views coincided with his. And firmly repressing the suspicion that this was just a little petty, Oriel got up and limped down the stairs. From now on she was not going to be picked up and carried around the place as if she were a doll. She would walk on her own, admittedly shaky, legs.

That way, the memory of the way his body moved against her, the unexpected sense of security she felt in his arms, could be quickly forgotten.

He surprised her again as she was picking another frangipani blossom. She said on an indrawn breath, 'You move like a cat. No noise at all.'

'It surprises you?'

'You're so big,' she said wryly. 'It doesn't seem natural. Big people are usually clumsy.'

Smiling, he took the flower from her. Cool, strong fingers tilted her chin. Her eyes closing against the dazzling sunlight, she felt his touch like arrows in her blood as he tucked the scented bloom into the thick, short curls above her ear.

'Size has little to do with strength or agility.'

'You're very strong too.' Her voice was quiet.

His thumb touched the throbbing curve of her mouth. Soft and persuasive, it was like a lover's caress. Her startled eyes widened for a second, before the heavy lids fell in unconscious provocation.

A muscle jerked in his jaw. The sun shaded the upper part of his face, but she could feel the burning silver gaze fixed on the soft width of her mouth, and she thought her lips stung. She was carried resistlessly by tides of sensation, partly the drowsy, drugging heat of the sun and the floating perfume of the flower, but more the surges of response in her, the primeval pull of attraction.

'I keep myself fit,' he said, his tone distant yet threaded with cool speculation. 'Speaking of which, would you like to go for a swim?'

I have to stop this! she thought. It took a will-power she hadn't even known she possessed, but she managed to drag her eyes from his face and step away, almost visibly gathering her self-control around her.

'I'd love to,' she said slowly, forcing her sluggish brain to work. 'Blaize, have you heard anything about David? I meant to ask before, but we got side-tracked.'

'Yes, I rang this morning,' His voice was crisp, almost dismissive. 'He's fine. In pain, I gather, but recovering. Tell me, what on earth were the pair of you doing roaming through the hills with a tropical storm on the rampage?'

'David decided we should go,' she said drily.

'So of course you went with him.'

Oddly cold but once more in control of her reactions, she looked about her. A seat under the pohutukawa tree on the edge of the beach beckoned. She said, 'Do you mind if I sit down over there?'

'Of course not. Do you want me to carry you?'

'No.' She set off quickly, desperate to get away from him before she made an even bigger fool of herself. Unfortunately he sat down next to her on the seat, surveying her with those hard, shrewd eyes.

A little nervously she said, 'David isn't noted for his enthusiasm for outdoor pursuits, so I was surprised when he wanted to come. Still, there was no reason why he shouldn't, apart from the fact that I don't like him much.'

His gaze sharpened. 'You don't like him much?'

'It's not absolutely obligatory to like your cousin——'

'Your cousin!' Sudden anger slashed through his eyes, but as quickly as it had come it vanished, leaving an odd, enigmatic smile curling the corners of his mouth. 'So he invited himself along,' he said softly. 'Perhaps he wanted to be more than just a cousin to you, Oriel.'

She had the distinct feeling that she was missing out on half of this equivocal conversation, but she had to laugh at that. 'Not David,' she said with such conviction that Blaize looked curiously at her, that calculating smile still very much in evidence.

'Why?'

'Because I'm three inches taller than he is. There's no way David would want a woman taller than he is. Besides,' she added cheerfully, 'we've hated each other since we first came back from Fiji. Until then he'd been the only grandchild, the golden hope for the future. Not that he had any reason to worry about my taking his place— my grandparents loved him besottedly until they died, and his mother can't see a flaw in his character.'

'But you can.'

'He's spoilt and arrogant and pigheaded!' she said brutally. 'But he is my cousin, so I could hardly turn him down when he wanted to come. Apart from anything else, it would have created a certain amount of unpleasantness in the family. At first everything went well. We tramped up from Whangaruru, and were on our way to Cape Brett lighthouse when we heard the weather forecast. We took a vote on it and decided to head back. Only David wanted to keep going. He had the father and mother of a row with just about everyone.' She sighed, continuing morosely, 'I should have known.'

'But you went with him, just the same.'

'I had to,' she said flatly. 'He's family, even if he is a pain. And he has no experience; if I'd let him go by himself he'd have probably ended up killing himself, and my aunt and my mother would never have forgiven me!'

'So as it was all he managed was a broken leg.' Blaize was leaning back in the cool shade, his expression aloof.

'Yes. He insisted on putting up the tent too close to the creek. It was partly my fault, because I didn't really think it would flood the way it did, so I didn't protest too loudly.'

'Normally you'd have been safe, but we've had so much rain this summer that there's no soakage left in the ground.'

She nodded. 'Yes, well, the flood came down when David was still in the tent.'

'He was damned lucky he didn't drown.'

'I know,' she said quietly. 'It took me a while to find him, and all the time I thought he'd be dead, and I wondered what on earth I was going to tell Aunt Kerry. Then I found him, and splinted the leg, and had to drag him up the hill, out of reach of any more water. Thank God he stayed unconscious for most of it, but I've been worried that I might have done him some irreparable damage.'

'No,' he said, his hand covering hers for a comforting moment. 'The doctor I spoke to said thanks to you and your presence of mind, he's in good condition. How old is he?'

'Twenty-two,' she said with a funny little grimace to hide the fact that her heart was speeding up. 'Fully grown, so he was heavy, but still an adolescent in lots of ways.'

'Why did he quarrel with the rest of the group?'

She wriggled her shoulders. 'Oh, he made a nuisance of himself with one of the women, and got slapped down very hard by both her and her boyfriend. After that, I think he was looking for a way out.' She directed a very clear gaze his way. 'He tends to react impulsively.'

'His stupidity and lack of maturity could have got you both killed.'

'Yes, well, don't think I won't point that out to him.'

He showed his teeth in a humourless smile. 'I might well do that too,' he said evenly.

Instinct told her that Blaize would be deadly, using his tongue to excoriating effect. 'It's not——' she began, feeling suddenly sorry for David, but fell silent under Blaize's quizzical gaze, for of course it *was* his business. Because of David's pettiness and self-indulgence, Blaize was now lumbered with a resident invalid.

Besides, she thought with a pang of cousinly irritation, it would do David good to be hauled over the coals by an expert. Over the years he'd got away with murder.

'I doubt if it'll do much good,' she said.

He lifted his brows but said nothing, and she looked away with dazzled eyes, concentrating hard on the quiet beauty of the setting. Two bush-covered arms of land, sombre even in the sunlight, held the bay in a protective embrace; against one of them a jacaranda flaunted what was left of its showy lilac flowers. To the north the peak of Purerua stood out against the burnished sky; between it and them several yachts moved infinitesimally over the glittering sea. A breeze purred softly among the leaves of the tree above them, turning them so that the silver backs gleamed like small fishes against the dark sea of the canopy. The tang of salt mingled with the scent of the frangipani and the smell of new-cut grass.

Oriel sighed. 'It's so beautiful,' she murmured.

'Whenever I come back home I think it's the most beautiful country in the world.'

She nodded. 'Do you go fishing much?'

He followed her line of sight to the launch, its out-riggers pointing at the sky. 'When I'm here, yes. I enjoy pitting my wits against the big fish. Then I tag them and let them go.'

She was glad. 'They're such beautiful creatures,' she said, unaware that something like wistfulness coloured her tones. 'So wild and free.'

Cynically, he observed, 'Nothing is free. Every organism is bound by the immutable laws of its existence. We think we are free, but it's an illusion.'

'That,' she said carefully, 'is an awfully depressing philosophy.'

He gave her a sardonic look. 'Do you think so? Tell me, why didn't you leave your cousin to find his own way back and stay with the group as you had originally intended?'

Her bottom lip jutted. Smiling slightly, he said, 'Because you're bound by the bonds of kinship and responsibility.'

She pondered on this for a few seconds, then said obstinately, 'But we have some free will.'

'Perhaps a child does, but the first thing good parents do is socialise their children so that they fit into the social system they are going to grow up in. A job taken on also by teachers like you. And when it's done, any hope of free will flies out of the window.'

She challenged him with a sideways tilt of her head. 'It has to be done. Humans are social animals, and they have to learn to fit in with the group.'

'I know. It's an interesting problem, isn't it? We need the close affection, the comradeship, the interaction with our fellows, yet deep in most people's hearts there's resentment at the ties and the responsibilities, the demands made on us by those people we love.'

'An interesting dichotomy,' she said, a sly note of humour colouring her tone.

He laughed, appreciating her amusement. 'Very interesting. I'm sure that's why the romance pedlars, those who say that one man and one woman can live happily ever after, are doomed to failure. Love begins in dependence, and it ends in resentment and the struggle to be free.'

'That is horribly cynical!'

He cocked an eyebrow. 'Waiting for your prince, Oriel?'

She responded to the lazy taunt in his voice with a shrug. 'Princes and princesses have never just come along. No, I'm not waiting. I enjoy my job, I like my life. If I want to get married I suppose I will one day, but I'm not actively seeking out good husband material.'

A large black-backed gull swooped over the garden, landed on the lawn and meditatively waddled across to a patch of sunlight beside a hibiscus bush. He stretched out a wing and preened, then tucked it back in and seemed to go to sleep, hunching his head down into his shoulders.

'Not a starry-eyed romantic?' Blaize said smoothly.

Oriel gave him a direct look. 'No, you're quite safe.'

He laughed, and after a moment, slightly startled at her own temerity, she joined in.

They sat in a silent but satisfying companionship for some minutes until he said, 'I'll get Kathy to find your bathing-suit and we'll go swimming. Pool or sea?'

'The sea,' she said instantly.

He nodded across the lawn to the stained wood summerhouse she had seen from the conservatory. 'There's a dressing-room there. Can you make it?'

'Yes, thank you.'

But he came with her, just the same. Once inside she looked around at the slatted floor and the shower, the handbasin and bath. Comparatively spartan compared to the house, it was still more than most seaside baches had. How much would it cost to keep the place running all year? As well as Kathy there was a gardener, and both would be in full-time employment to keep the house and its environs so immaculate. Yet it was a holiday house.

Her musings were interrupted by Kathy, carrying the bathing-suit. 'Can I help you get into it?' she asked, seeing that Oriel had made no effort to strip off her sun-dress.

Oriel smiled. 'No, I can manage.'

'It shouldn't be hard. I got it with the zip down the front so it would be easy to manage.'

It was, but Oriel frowned uncomfortably as she looked at herself in the mirror. The suit was cut high in the legs, but she was used to that. It was low-necked, but she was accustomed to that too. What caught her eyes was the colour, hot pink with a black panel up the front, and in the middle of that the zip, pink again, that extended from below her navel to the neckline.

Even fully pulled up it was—provocative, she decided, frowning as she fiddled with the fastener. Slowly she eased it down a couple of inches. Like that it revealed the small swells of her breasts and became downright challenging. Setting her lips, she hauled it up and grabbed her towel.

It took quite a bit of will-power to make her way through the door and out across the grass, and more was needed when she saw Blaize leaning against a great branch of the pohutukawa, obviously waiting for her.

He straightened as she came towards him. Unease rippled like the touch of a wet cloth across her skin, pulling it tight, standing the tiny hairs on end. Beneath that silent, enigmatic regard she felt acutely self-conscious, aware as never before of the tiny changes in her body that signalled, she realised with an odd sort of shame, arousal.

He said nothing, and she was too unsure of herself to be able to think of something that might defuse the unexpected, shattering tension. He was wearing dark blue racing briefs, and he was magnificent, the splendid muscles of his body sleek and taut beneath skin like bronze, oiled silk, his body hair describing a tree-of-life pattern across his chest.

As she came up to him he smiled, a tiny movement of his beautiful mouth that was totally without humour. 'Kathy chose well. How old are you, Oriel?'

She answered curtly, wondering why telling him her age was some sort of betrayal. 'Twenty-three.'

'I had thought you younger.' He held out his hand.

She didn't want to take it—the last thing she wanted to do was touch him—but she couldn't manage the steep, short path down to the beach alone. With immense reluctance she accepted his help, taking a short, impeded breath as his strong fingers closed warmly over hers.

He said nothing as he supported her down the bank beneath the black shade of the pohutukawa, and came out into the brilliant glare of the sun. The glittering sand seared the tender skin of her arches. She stopped.

Without a word he picked her up, the long, heavily muscled thighs flexing, the dense, fine hair on his chest and arms brushing sensually against her thin, hot skin. She held herself rigidly as he strode across the blazing beach down to the thick, cool sand left by the receding tide, and into the crisp little waves.

When the waves creamed around his lean waist he released her. Of course she had to stumble, her hands shooting out to clutch at his arms, then falling away in embarrassment. His finger came up, touched the round loop at the end of the zip.

'I wonder,' he said ironically, 'if Kathy realised just how provocative that bathing-suit would be when she bought it.'

Oriel flushed. 'No, she got it because it's easier to put on and take off.'

'Exactly,' he said in a voice so dry that it took her a moment to understand.

She looked up into the polished opacity of his eyes. Colour washed across her cheekbones as his mouth pulled in at the corners. Awkwardly she turned away, her emotions rubbed raw by the tension between them, the spark of sensual fire that had its inception in the first long look they had taken at each other up in her bedroom.

Accustomed to hiding her emotions, she was sure she could cope with this new set, strange and powerful though they were. But he felt it too. That narrowed, burning gaze, the almost tangible air of intense absorption that emanated from him, meant that he too was in thrall to that most primitive of summonses.

And something else was happening to her. Although he wasn't touching her, wasn't even very close, her breasts seemed to expand, become heavier, and to her astonishment she felt a strange pulling sensation in the nipples. Intuition hurtled her into the water, hiding the betrayal of her body in the cool refuge of the sea.

Because of her excellent lung capacity she came up some distance away, water dripping from her face as she pushed the heavy locks back from her eyes and drew in a deep breath as she trod water. His shout froze her; she obeyed his imperative command by coming reluctantly back in, stopping a sensible distance away, well out of reach.

Anger sculpted his features into a primitive mask. In a toneless voice he said, 'Don't ever do that again. You haven't checked the bottom for rocks, you have no idea of the hazards.'

She bit her lip. Normally she would have been much more careful. 'I keep my eyes open underwater,' she offered as a sop.

He stared her down. 'Don't do it again.'

'All right, I won't. Are there any rocks?'

'A clump in the centre of the bay, about two hundred metres out.' He pointed to a dark shadow. 'They're about five feet under when the tide's dead low. Stay away from them.'

Nodding, she went under again, then surfaced and began to free-style back and forth across the bay, trying to exhaust the strange energy that streamed through her body in an electric current.

She ignored Blaize. Or rather, they ignored each other. As much at home in the water as she was, he swam almost out to the mouth of the bay. Once she paused and watched the strong bronzed arms cleaving the water as though he too were in flight from demons. He looked antique, from beyond time; she thought fancifully that dolphins should accompany him, nymphs and tritons beckon him through the fascinating sunlit seas of pagan Greece.

After twenty minutes she came out, and by the time he emerged she had showered and was lying on her back on a lounger, trying very hard to make some sense of what was happening to her. Although she didn't enjoy the sensations that rioted through her at Blaize's touch, she couldn't discipline a certain hidden, sly pride that rejoiced because her body had the power to invoke a response from him.

This pleasure in her femininity was new to her. She had been so tall and lanky in her adolescence that she had towered over all her classmates. The few boys she had met made it more than obvious that they were not interested in someone so much taller than they. Her mother had insisted on excellent posture, for which she was now grateful, but she had grown up thinking herself lacking in any feminine attraction that might interest the opposite sex.

But Blaize was attracted to her, she could sense it, and her body responded like a well-fed cat with a feline satisfaction in its own sensuality that was as alarming as it was exhilarating.

Which explained why she was lying out on the terrace instead of hiding in her room, and why, when she sensed his arrival, she smiled and said sleepily, 'Thank heavens summer's here at last. I thought we might have tropical storms until winter arrived.'

'We still might,' he returned somewhat grimly. 'The long-range forecast is not hopeful. However, we'll enjoy this while we can.'

Did his tone invest the words with a hidden meaning? Suddenly appalled at her behaviour, she refused to look at him, turning over on to her front so that he couldn't see her face. How stupid she was to think a man like Blaize Stephenson would be interested in her! It was mortifying to realise that she was behaving like some teenager in the throes of a massive crush, cheapening herself.

But she jumped violently, her lashes flying up, when she felt his hand on her shoulder.

'If you're going to sit like that, you need sunscreen,' he said, the comment like a taunt as his hand smoothed icy liquid over her skin.

Reading scorn in his expression, she returned gracelessly, 'I can do it.'

His nearness was suffocating. He was laughing at her, she could tell, but he handed the plastic bottle over and sat down himself, not on the chair next to her, but on her lounger, presenting the broad expanse of his back to her. 'Then do mine, will you?'

No doubt in his circles everyone rubbed sunscreen promiscuously all over everybody else, she thought feverishly. Of course they did; she had done it frequently herself, a simple service performed in a spirit of friendship, or common humanity, or something. Why then did she feel as though if she laid a finger on him she was going to fall off a cliff and never find her way back up again?

Because she was an idiot in the throes of her first sexual passion, and she was coping with it with all of the *savoir-faire* of the average fourteen-year-old, clogged with hormones and inhibitions. Scolding herself, she took a deep breath, squirted a palmful of clear liquid on to her hand and tentatively lifted it to his back.

His skin was smooth and warm and still damp from the sea, sliding easily beneath her tentative fingers, which moved over the highlighted muscles and tendons that made men so fascinatingly different from women. Smoothing the lotion over him came disturbingly close to a caress.

Thank heavens he wasn't able to see her face! She banished all expression from it and said in a voice that sounded astoundingly like hers, 'There, that should do it.'

'Thank you.'

He got up while she anointed her own shoulders and arms, then he slathered the clear liquid down the long golden length of her calves.

'I'll take the bandage off,' he said, and did so, then ran his hand up to her calf and smoothed the residue of sunscreen down over her ankle and foot.

His touch ricocheted through her body, sending secret messages singing through every nerve and cell in an arcane temptation that could destroy her if she listened to it.

'Thank you,' she said through stiff lips as she screwed the top back on the bottle and put it on the table.

He sat down in a chair which gave him a clear view of her face. She waited warily, acutely conscious of the unrelenting impact of his scrutiny, afraid to meet it.

'My nephew and niece arrive tomorrow,' he said, when she was almost quivering with tension.

'Really? I didn't know it was tomorrow they were coming.' Oh, brilliant, she thought with disgust.

'They had Christmas with their father's parents in Wellington, so I've no doubt they'll arrive spoilt.'

She smiled a little wistfully. Her grandparents had died so long ago she could only just remember them. 'That's what grandparents are for, I believe. To spoil their grandchildren.'

'These ones are inclined to overdo it—materially, at least,' he said drily. 'They tend to be a little old-fashioned in their outlook, and demand a very high standard of behaviour, rewarding the children with expensive gifts. I suppose they want to compensate for their loss, but there must be a happy medium.'

Something in his very lack of emotion registered. Impulsively she leaned over and put her slim, strong hand over his. When she realised what she was doing she tried to yank it back, but his turned and caught hers in his strong clasp.

Without looking at her he said, still in that same unnaturally level voice, 'Jim was their only child, Sue my only sister. We had no brothers. They were young and very much in love. He was a lawyer—they had everything to live for. But some criminally stupid idiot bought himself a cruiser he couldn't control and took it out at the back of Rangitoto, drank himself into sottish irresponsibility and ran them down.'

Horrified, she whispered, 'I'm so sorry. It's an utterly useless thing to say, but I am.'

'The children were on the beach,' he went on tonelessly. 'They saw it happen. The friends they were with said Jim and Sue yelled—then they dived, but the boat went straight over the top of them.'

She twined her hands around his, seeking to give him some comfort, something to allay the hell of emptiness she saw in the crystalline depths of his eyes. 'Poor kids,' she whispered. 'Blaize, I know there doesn't seem to be a reason for such tragedies, but...'

He lifted her hands to his mouth and kissed the tense fingers, before putting them back in her lap. He was in control, the awful darkness replaced by something she didn't understand until he spoke, very gently.

'It happened because a man arrogantly thought he had the right to indulge himself wherever he wanted to,' he said. 'Where he is now there are very few ways he can indulge himself, and when he comes out of prison there will be nothing left for him. As quickly and easily as he murdered my sister and her husband I've demolished the little financial empire he built, and there is no way he'll ever be able to build it again. He'll have difficulty finding the money to buy himself one drink.'

Revenge. Even unspoken, the word was ugly in the bright air, darkening the summer coast about them with its connotations. Oriel's skin tightened, the little hairs standing on end. She had been more correct than she knew when she'd called him pagan. The impulses that had fuelled the Greek tragedies lived on in him, crying for appeasement.

At the twist of his smile her protest died on her tongue. Confronted by his implacable will, she could only shiver.

'You don't approve? No, of course you don't. You were trained to be compassionate.' He got to his feet, looking down at her shrinking length with cold, controlled lack of interest. 'I had a different education,' he said calmly, and left her.

Oriel was in her room getting ready for dinner, her mind never wandering far from that lethal little scene, when the door opened and a child wandered in, a girl of about seven, well-built, with blue eyes and an aristocratic little nose above a wide, sweet mouth.

'Hello,' she said. 'What did you do to your foot?'

Oriel turned and smiled. 'I stupidly stepped into a deep hole and fell very awkwardly. You must be Sarah. I'm Oriel Radford.'

'Our plane got to Auckland early and there wasn't anyone to meet us, but Simon rang one of Uncle Blaize's men and he came out and brought us all the way up in his car.'

'What an adventure!'

This was clearly a new way of looking at matters. Sarah sat down on the bed and watched with interested eyes as Oriel dragged a comb through her hair, trying somewhat vainly to control the curls.

'Uncle Blaize was cross,' Sarah informed her, adding with relish, 'He said someone had made a mistake and Simon said heads would roll.'

Oriel said calmly, 'I doubt it. Everyone makes mistakes sometimes.'

'Well, Uncle Blaize will pay back whoever was wrong,' Sarah responded, charming Oriel with a tentative, endearingly gappy smile. 'Can I watch you put your make-up on?'

Oriel made a face at her in the mirror. 'I haven't got any to put on, so I'm afraid the answer has to be no.'

'Not even some lipstick?' True feminine horror coloured the child's expression.

Turning around, Oriel touched the pale, silky hair. 'No, not a skerrick. You see, I was tramping when I hurt my foot, and the only make-up you need tramping is sunscreen.'

'My mummy would take lipstick everywhere.' There was a wobble in the child's voice that wrung Oriel's heart. However, it was rapidly controlled. Sarah went on, 'Uncle Blaize said you aren't going to be able to walk for a whole month. Will you stay here all the time?'

'No. Why?'

'I just wondered,' she said vaguely, and then, 'My gov'ness just got married.'

Realising that the child had taken one of childhood's rapid shines to her, Oriel smiled sympathetically. 'I have to go back home as soon as my mother comes back from her holiday in Australia.'

Sarah sighed, and curled up on the bed, fixing Oriel with a penetrating gaze that reminded her of Blaize. 'I can't read.'

'Oh. Does it hurt?'

A sudden giggle transformed the carefully blank expression. 'No, don't be silly, of course it doesn't, but I have to learn how to soon, 'cause I'm backward.'

'Who said that?' Oriel was swept by a wave of cold anger.

'My gran told my grandad. And she said my gov'ness told her. I need specialist attention. What's backward? And what's attention?'

'Attention is what I'm giving you, listening to someone carefully, and backward means that you need a little more attention than other children.'

Sarah sighed. ''Cause I'm dumb. I'm in the bottom group at school.'

'You don't sound dumb to me,' Oriel said cautiously, 'and I should know, because I'm a teacher.'

'Are you?' Sarah eyed her warily, before asking. 'Do you like being a teacher?'

'Very much. Mostly, anyway.'

'What don't you like about it?'

Blaize answered from the door. 'Children who don't stop asking questions. Come on, Sarah, your dinner's ready.'

Racing across the room, she lifted a rapturous little face to him. 'Can't I have it with you?'

'Not tonight.' He touched her cheek with a gentle hand. 'Early to bed this evening; tomorrow you'll be able to stay up a little later.'

Her bottom lip thrust out. 'It's not fair! Simon's staying up tonight, why can't I? You never let me——'

'That's enough.'

There was just enough sharpness in the injunction to stop the whining outburst, not so much that it upset an already tired child. Oriel applauded his tactics silently as he smiled teasingly down at his niece, unsurprised when an answering smile glimmered in the large eyes, magically banishing the sulkiness.

'Oh, all right,' she said offhandedly, tucking her small paw in his. 'Promise to come up and read me a story?'

He contrived to look offended. 'Do I ever miss?'

'Sometimes you're not there, and anyway, Gran says I'm too old for that now.'

Oriel's eyes met Blaize's. For a moment the polished pewter was pierced by anger, until he said in a noncommittal voice, 'Well, I'm here tonight, and I don't think you're too old for it.'

Sarah smiled worshipfully up at him. 'Simon doesn't either. He tucked me up while I was there.' Remembering her manners, she turned and said politely, 'It was nice to meet you, Oriel.' She skipped through the door and off down the stairs.

Blaize turned a detached gaze on Oriel. 'You seem to get on like a house on fire.'

'She's a dear little girl.'

He nodded. 'I think so. Come on down and meet Simon.' His eyes fell to her foot. 'Do you want me to carry you?'

She shook her head. 'No, it's all right.'

He insisted on accompanying her down the stairs, and although he watched her closely enough to bring the fugitive colour to her cheeks, she couldn't rid herself of the suspicion that the quick, clever brain was busy with plans and schemes in which she didn't figure at all.

CHAPTER FOUR

Simon was a tall boy with his sister's blue eyes, hands and feet that seemed too large for him, and a pleasant smile, although he looked a little surprised at his first glimpse of Oriel. No doubt, she thought cynically, she was not the sort of woman he was accustomed to seeing with Blaize.

He had charming manners, however, and a hint of the lazy smile that his uncle used so successfully, and within a few minutes she decided she liked him very much. She lost her normal air of slight reserve, and with a skill that was partly taught but mostly inborn set herself to easing his diffidence, while Blaize looked on with avuncular, but faintly derisive, satisfaction.

That evening set the tone for the days that followed. Sarah attached herself to Oriel, spending long hours talking to her or playing with the litter of kittens that lived in the corner of the garage, while Simon enjoyed himself swimming and water-skiing, diving and fishing and exploring, often with Blaize, but also with the family of the farm manager—a son and two daughters who were a match for both boys.

Kathy, beginning to organise the party at the end of the holidays, shooed Oriel outside when she asked if she could help. 'The greatest help you can give me,' she said with a meaning nod at Sarah, 'is to keep that one busy and out of my kitchen.'

So they spent a lot of time together. There could hardly have been a greater contrast than between the cheerful, extroverted boy and his sister, who betrayed her insecurity in almost every remark she made.

Oriel understood Sarah's deep-rooted fears, the whining and clinging that sometimes marked her behaviour, her frightened dependence on her brother and her uncle. From the few remarks she made about her father's parents it seemed that they were older and stiffer, with outdated ideas of child-rearing and an emphasis on stiff upper lips that discounted the little girl's grief.

Oriel's too tender heart ached for her, especially on the days when she was left behind, staring morosely as the deep-sea fishing boat took her brother and uncle out to the fishing grounds.

'It's not fair!' she wailed. 'Uncle Blaize is *mean*! Why can't I go with them? I could take a pill like I do when I go in the plane.'

'And then you'd be too dozy to enjoy yourself, love.'

'Yes, but Simon can do anything he likes, and I have to stay here all the time. It's not *fair*!'

Oriel slanted an amused glance at her. After a moment the petulant little face relaxed. 'You talk with your eyes,' Sarah accused, but she was smiling. 'How do you do that? Uncle Blaize talks with his eyes too. I want to talk with my eyes.'

Yes, Blaize certainly spoke with his eyes. And perhaps his most infuriating communication was the cool, bland irony that she so often met now. Aloud, Oriel said, 'You do, sweetheart. Everyone does.'

Sarah found this idea interesting, and spent some time conveying messages with her eyes for Oriel to decode. However, too soon she relapsed back into crossness.

'I'm bored,' she announced, kicking at the leg of her chair. 'Aren't you bored too, Oriel?'

Bored? No, she wasn't bored. Just a little flat. And the silly, shameful reason for that was that as well as being avuncular to the children, Blaize was acting like an uncle to her too. Small shivers still ran across her skin when she saw him, when he gave her one of his lazy smiles, but clearly her presence no longer affected him in the least.

If it ever had. Perhaps he had just pretended... Or perhaps he had not intended to expose as much of his character as he had with those last frightening revelations. Would she ever forget the note in his voice when he told her what he was doing to the man who had killed his sister? She shivered. She had sensed that he was formidable, but not that he was truly dangerous. Sophisticated and enigmatic, almost too handsome to be taken seriously, beneath that worldly exterior was a merciless strength and a controlled, uncompromising instinct for revenge.

'Are you bored, Oriel?' Sarah persisted.

'No. I'm enjoying a lovely, lazy holiday in superb weather with a friend I like very much. I'm not bored.'

Sarah sighed. 'Not even just a tiny little bit? Wouldn't you like to get up and walk around?'

'Yes, but if I do my foot swells up and gets sore again, so it's not worth it.'

'You're lucky, you can read.' Sarah's eyes lingered on the book that lay closed on Oriel's slim lap. 'Could you teach me to read, Oriel? Now?'

Carefully Oriel replied, 'If you really want to learn, and really want to work, yes.'

Too many rebuffs, too much disillusion, rendered the sun-kissed little face cautious. Sighing, Sarah looked up into Oriel's eyes. 'I do want to read, more than anything in the whole world, so Simon and Uncle Blaize can be proud of me.'

'Darling, they love you very much,' Oriel said gently.

'I know, but I want them to be *proud* of me.'

'I'm sure they're very proud of you.'

But Sarah knew better. 'They'll be proud of me when I read,' she said. 'Will you teach me, Oriel?'

There could be only one reply to this. Crossing her fingers behind her back, Oriel said confidently, 'Yes, of course. Go and get me one of your story-books, love, one that you like, and a pencil and some paper.'

By now convinced that Sarah was definitely not backward, Oriel knew she had very little time to find out what exactly was causing the block, and she hoped fervently that she would be able to help the child.

When Sarah reappeared she came across the lawn with a set look on her small face that upset Oriel more than anything she had seen before. The child looked hopeless, beaten before she started.

However, after half an hour Oriel was feeling much more confident. It now seemed almost certain that most of Sarah's trouble was psychological, her conviction that she was backward being the main cause of her difficulties. Oriel thought dark thoughts of grandparents who spoke out of turn. And somewhere along the way the child had missed out on any grounding in phonics.

It was on this lack that Oriel based her plan. A knowledge of phonics would not automatically produce a reader, but it would give the child confidence and a method of attack she could use when confronted with a new word. Above all, Oriel knew, she would have to rebuild the confidence that had been lost.

They worked until lunchtime, and again for a couple of hours in the afternoon, but when Sarah began making mistakes Oriel said firmly, 'Right, that's it. You're too tired.'

Sarah protested, 'But I want to learn some more.'

'I'm tired, and hot, and thirsty, which means you are too. When people get tired they start to make mistakes. Too much is as bad as too little, my friend. Do you think you could give me a hand up the steps to the terrace? My foot's aching a little. Then we can have a swim.'

Sarah was sympathetic, but she was not one to give in immediately. Even as she put a hand to help Oriel up she persisted, 'Can we do some more after dinner?'

Oriel smiled, smoothing the flyaway hair from the flushed little brow. 'No, love, we can't. The men will be back then, and didn't you say you want to keep it a secret?'

'Oh, yes, I forgot. It's easier when you teach me, Oriel. Us'ly I feel sick when I have to read and I can't do it, and the teacher's words all get mixed up. Miss Kaye used to get mad with me when I made mistakes and say I didn't try, but I did. Everything just all mixed up together. You don't growl when I make mistakes, and I don't make so many.'

She gave Oriel a swift, fervent hug and was off, no doubt to confide her secret to the kittens. Oriel watched her with darkened eyes, deciding to talk to Blaize about specialist help for his niece.

After dinner Simon went off to brag to his new-found friends about the marlin he had caught and tagged, and for the first time in days Oriel found herself sitting out alone on the terrace beside Blaize. It was a glorious night, warm and heavily scented with frangipani and gardenia and the heavy musk of the Queen of the Night. Overhead the stars blazed fiercely, while in the east a luminous sky presaged a moonrise later. Oriel listened to the hush of the waves, as sensuous as the rustle of silk about white limbs, and the call of the morepork from one of the bush-clad headlands.

'I hear you're teaching Sarah how to read.'

She turned a surprised face to the dark silhouette of the man in the chair beside her. 'Who told you?'

His teeth flashed momentarily in the starshine. 'Sarah, of course, in strictest confidence.'

Her laughter was muted. 'So much for secrecy!'

'She's not noted for keeping secrets.' His voice hardened. 'Do you think you can do it?'

Her shoulders moved a little uneasily. 'I think so. Oh, not to read properly, but I can give some sort of grounding and help build her confidence. That's her main problem.' Without condemnation she told him of the grandparents' overheard conversation.

'Their son was their only child, and so Simon is the only grandson. He has always been quick and bright, a handsome, winning child. I'm afraid Sarah wasn't accepted for her own loving little self. They wanted another Simon.'

'It happens,' she agreed, thinking of her mother, who would have been much happier with a bright, handsome son.

'I know. It made no difference to Sue, but Jim was disappointed in Sarah's progress. Simon taught himself to read when he was four; he was fluent before he went to school. When it became obvious that Sarah wasn't going to do the same, it was commented on.'

'Did your sister try to teach her how to read?'

'I think she did. How did you know?'

'Guessed,' she sighed. 'Poor little Sarah—the more she failed the harder it was for her to believe that she could do it. It happens. Teachers do their best, but with big classes they can only do so much.'

'She went to a private school. And to a specialist who was supposed to help her.'

'Thereby reinforcing her conviction that she was a failure.'

His voice very hard, he said, 'And if you fail it will further reinforce it.'

Oriel braced herself. 'I won't fail,' she said with the utmost conviction. 'She's taken a fancy to me, which is half the battle. And she's ready to learn now. She asked me to teach her. Also, this is about as far removed from a school as any place could be.'

'She hasn't been to school for the last term. She was so shattered by her parents' death that she was unable to cope with a normal classroom, so I've kept her at home with a governess, who didn't seem to be able to get through to her at all. Are you sure you can do it?'

She didn't blame him for the disbelief in his tone, but she knew she was a good teacher, and she trusted her instincts where Sarah was concerned. 'Not so she's fluent, no, but I can give her confidence, get her to the stage where she can see results. If you get a sympathetic teacher to build on that, she'll catch up with her peer group. She's as bright as a button, and she'd not dyslexic, which worried me a little. I think she's recovering from the shock of her parents' death and is ready. I happened to be near at the appropriate moment when she made the decision for herself.'

'I see.' He was silent for a few seconds before commanding, 'Tell me how you plan to deal with her.'

She explained, her voice assured and calmly confident. He listened attentively, occasionally asking an intelligent question, accepting her answers, clearly respecting her expertise.

'So you think she's made a breakthrough?'

'I hope so. Which reminds me, I've made a short list of books I could use with her. When someone goes into town next, could they get them?'

'Yes, of course.'

She nodded and got to her feet, aware of the undercurrents that had run deep and threatening all through the conversation, even when they had been talking of Sarah. Now that she had slipped out of her professional persona she could feel his attention like a lick of fire across her skin.

From the depths of his chair he said, 'You obviously like her.'

'Yes, she's a nice kid. Very affectionate, but with enough ginger to liven her up and a surprising amount of will-power. She'll be all right.'

'Do you realise that she wants you to be her new governess?'

Astonishment held her silent. Then she smiled rather sadly. 'I suppose it was inevitable. Never mind, she'll get over it.'

'Not that governess is really an apt description of the job,' he said as though she hadn't spoken. 'Sarah needs stability and love. The last governess was efficient, but she wasn't able to engage Sarah's affections.' His voice was level and expressionless, but it was clear that he had not liked the last governess.

Oriel sat down again, conscious of the dull throb of her foot. Bending, she loosened the bandage. Her eyes had adjusted to the starshine and she could see his face, angular and bold, Viking-strong in the night. An odd little *frisson* snaked down her spine, similar to awareness yet subtly different, with an undertone of foreboding.

'Then you'll have to let her choose the next one herself,' she said in her soft, pleasant voice.

Again that lazy smile. 'I think she already has,' he pointed out calmly.

Sheer astonishment robbed her of words. At last she stammered, 'M-me? Oh, no, I couldn't!'

'Why not?' He was inexorable. 'She needs someone she's fond of, who will like her. She needs reassurance. I'll pay a respectable wage, better than you can get teaching, and you'll travel too. You might even be able to get back to Fiji—I have interests there.'

'It sounds marvellous,' she said quietly, her stupid heart breaking, breaking, breaking. For of course this was why he had been so charming, so pleasant—and lately, so aloof. He wanted someone to look after his niece.

'Then take it.'

'I can't.' Wildly she searched for an excuse to soften the blunt refusal. 'I can't let my headmistress down. She probably won't be able to find a replacement.'

He laughed, cynicism personified. 'Your headmistress has a relieving teacher who is prepared to take your position for the rest of the year.'

'But—how——?' She stopped, dragging a hand through her hair. For a moment her thought processes jammed, then were galvanised into action by outrage and hurt. 'You have no right to go behind my back!' she flashed. 'How dare you treat me like a puppet, to be manipulated into doing what you want? You have a damned nerve, but fortunately I don't have to put up with it!'

He rose from the chair with the leashed power and menace of a predator intent on blood, holding her still by the simple expedient of clamping his hands on her shoulders. She staggered, and had to grasp his wrists to steady herself.

'What a temper!' he marvelled, not at all intimidated. 'No, you can't storm off in a huff, Oriel, not unless you want to come a cropper. Sit down and be sensible.'

He was smooth-talking her. His hands slid down to her waist, burning through the fine cotton shirt until she regained her balance. The breath still came racing through her lips, but for a different reason now. Angry as she still was, his closeness excited her, as did the feel of his hands almost spanning her narrow waist in a grip that was as intimate as it was unbearable. So close, he blocked out the stars and the sea, filling her whole world.

Frustrated and a little frightened by her body's treachery, she muttered, 'You have no right——'

He broke in with smooth amusement. 'Listen to me, you little spitfire. I have not manipulated you. I merely anticipated what your objections would be and saved time by forestalling them. Sarah needs you more than any of the children in your class. She'll repay you tenfold for your affection and your efforts with her.' His voice deepened into warm persuasion. 'She needs your warmth and your practical sympathy, your companionship and your love. You know what it's like to lose a dearly loved parent. Her previous governess made no secret of the fact that she thought her a whiny, spoilt little object. You know exactly how to handle her, and she's already halfway to loving you.'

He was working seductive magic on her heart-strings. Oh, he was clever, she though distantly. Somehow he had discerned that she was hungry for someone to love, and he was using that weakness to play on her sympathy. Unfortunately, although she knew exactly what he was doing, she was half convinced that she could give Sarah what she needed.

His voice was that of the tempter—smooth, reasonable, with secret, hidden aims. If she took the job would she be laying up heartbreak for herself? What she felt for him now was merely a physical attraction, the appeal of a virile man for a nubile woman; he too felt it, the common coinage of desire between male and female. But he controlled his appetites, they did not control him. He was able to subdue them if they became inconvenient, as he had the minute it had occurred to that calculating, clever mind that she would make Sarah an excellent governess. If she left now she would have little to recover from—a few tense moments, a little flirtation, a ruffle of awareness, that was all.

But if she stayed, seeing him all the time, in effect sharing a house with him, would this juvenile crush deepen and mature to another, more painful emotion, one he could not return?

Frowning, she looked away, trying to rid her mind of the slow, sweet lure of temptation. Clear thought was impossible when her senses were stirring like this.

She swallowed and said quietly, 'I can't decide—I need to think it over.'

From a distance she heard him say, 'All right, then, give me your decision tomorrow.'

'Tomorrow?' she said indignantly.

'A good night's sleep is supposed to give good counsel, isn't it? Think it over before you go to sleep and let your subconscious decide.'

The arrogant confidence in his voice stiffened her backbone. In a cool, crisp voice she asked, 'Where exactly would we live?'

'I have three main bases,' he said, just as though he hadn't won a minor victory. 'The house in Auckland, one just outside London, and an apartment in New York. I try to spend most of the holidays here with the children, but I travel a fair amount, although I'm cutting down on that as much as I can.'

She said in a stunned voice, 'Who are you?'

He paused, as though the question had surprised him. Then in a neutral voice he said, 'I'm a businessman. My grandfather started from this farm and built a pastoral empire in New Zealand and Australia, with interests further afield in tea plantations and rubber. My father expanded into manufacturing; I'm interested in commercial property.'

'Stephensons,' she said in a stunned voice. Of course, that was where she had seen his name, in innumerable newspapers, in prestigious magazines, on lists of huge, wealthy organisations. Blaize Stephenson was not just a businessman, he was a magnate, courted by governments, wooed by countries, respected for his extraordinary knack of making money and the immense power he wielded.

'Yes.'

Round and golden as a grapefruit, the moon sprang up from the sea, silhouetting the broad shoulders wide enough to take the burdens of a vast international organisation. How could she have been so blind?

She said baldly, 'I don't think——'

'Go to bed, Oriel. It's getting late and you're tired. Do you want me to carry you up?'

His voice was autocratic, the voice of a man who commanded power and authority. She said hastily, 'No. I can walk, thank you. Goodnight.'

'Goodnight,' he said with cool self-possession. Before she reached the house he was walking across the lawn towards the beach.

Simon emerged from the depths of the television-room as she made her way to the stairs; grinning, he offered to help her up, and she saw in the laughing boy's face some of the physical attraction of the man outside.

'What makes the men of this family think they can pick me up and carry me about all the time?' she said, striving for lightness. 'I'd give you a hernia.'

He grinned again. 'Oh, I was thinking more of putting my arm around your waist,' he told her outrageously, then blushed at her spontaneous peal of laughter.

'Grateful though I am for you offer, I'll pass,' she told him.

'Well, OK, but I can help if you'd like me to.'

'It's fine, it's not really painful.'

But she was glad to get into bed and rest her foot. Unfortunately, rest did not come so easily to her brain. She lay for hours wondering just what she should do, whether the risk was worth the reward, then slipped so smoothly into sleep that it was morning before she was aware of it.

Blaize might feel that her subconscious knew best, but hers seemed as much a ditherer as its owner. She woke early, and lay watching the sun come up over the hills behind the bay, her thoughts confused and tangled. One part of her, the sensible part, warned her that she was walking into danger if she even thought of giving up her safe job, a life that she enjoyed, for the unknown prospects of life shared with the most exciting, most charismatic man she had ever met.

Her discovery of Blaize's identity frightened her. If she had been harbouring secret hopes and dreams, his revelation last night had put paid to them with casual finality. Blaize Stephenson, farmer or businessman, might perhaps fall in love with Oriel Radford. But Blaize Stephenson, head of a worldwide organisation, old money, the darling of the financial pages as owner of one of the few businesses that had come unscathed through the share-market collapse, that Blaize Stephenson was so far out of her reach that he might as well be Prince Charles.

So would she get over this inconvenient crush?

Because there was no doubt that he had seen her as a suitable prospect for the job, if not right from the start, then almost immediately. It hurt, but she had to admit that he hadn't capitalised on the sexual attraction between them. He could have, but he clearly had standards and a moral code.

Should she exchange a life that was pleasant but a little mundane for another that would be infinitely more exciting? At least until Sarah was old and secure enough to go to boarding-school. The prospect of seeing the world was very desirable; for a while she managed to fool herself that that was what really appealed to her.

Because she wasn't in love with Blaize—she wasn't so stupid. He was too old for her, emotionally if not physically, too cynical. It was just the first time she had been in contact with a man of such blazing sexual charisma. Of course she would get over this—this clamour in the blood. It would die from lack of nourishment. And would she ever feel happy again if she ignored Sarah's silent pleas for help, her deep-seated need for a mother figure?

Just think, she adjured herself, how sick you would be if you decided not to do it! You would really be angry with yourself for turning down this wonderful opportunity. After all, her father had left Great Britain for the South Seas—surely there was a little of the same adventurous spirit in her?

It was this final thought that made up her mind. As she made her way carefully down the stairs, she had a final pang of uncertainty, one she squashed firmly. It was too late.

'Oriel, wait for me!' Sarah called, bouncing and smiling as she ran along the passage. 'Oriel, Uncle Blaize says you're going to come and be my governess. Is he right?'

Oriel was furious at this blatant pre-emption of her decision but she managed to hide it from the child, who grabbed her hand and was gazing up with such hopeful eyes.

'Yes,' she said, smiling. 'Do you like the idea?'

Sarah gave a half-sob and flung her arms around her, clutching her with a hint of desperation. 'Forever?' she demanded. 'Promise to stay with me forever?'

'Forever is a long time,' Oriel said simply. She hesitated a second, then promised, 'For as long as you need me, sweetheart.' Not even to herself was she prepared to admit just how seriously she made the vow.

Sarah whooped with delight. 'Can I tell Simon?' she asked eagerly.

'Of course you can.'

Simon and Blaize were at breakfast in the morning-room. The sun was shining in across the tiled floor, and with the doors wide open the mingled scents of the garden and the sea wafted in on the lazy air; it was the epitome of summer living.

'Guess what, Simon?' Sarah cried importantly. 'Oriel's going to be my new governess. She's going to live with Uncle Blaize and me and teach me how to read!'

Simon looked startled, then smiled and said heartily, 'Hey, that's choice.'

'That's *what*?'

He laughed at Blaize's lifted brow and amended it to, 'Good, fine, neat, wonderful. Welcome to the family, Oriel.' Faint dismay crossed his face. 'Or will I have to call you Miss Radford, like we did Miss Kaye?'

'No, I'd prefer Oriel,' she said firmly, sliding into the chair Blaize held for her.

He said dulcetly, 'I'll see you in the office after breakfast, Oriel, if that's all right with you. We have a few things to discuss.'

The 'few things' turned out to be a contract which stated that she would stay in his employ for three months, and after that a binding decision would be made. It stipulated a salary about twice as much as she was getting as a teacher; when she jibbed he said calmly, 'But you won't just be a teacher, remember. You're going to have the responsibility for keeping Sarah happy as well. Believe me, she's been on her best behaviour with you so far—she can be a little brat. It won't be a sinecure.'

'Well, all right,' she said dubiously, and read through the rest of the paper. It stipulated her hours of freedom: two days a week off, and a month's holiday each year. For a moment she hesitated. It suddenly seemed a crazy thing to do, throw up everything she had worked for on the off chance that she would like acting as a mother to a child she barely knew. Then her promise and Sarah's ecstatic delight flashed into her mind. Her teeth sank into her lip; she drew a deep breath and with a hand that trembled only a little signed the sheet of paper.

'Right,' he drawled. 'You will, of course, remain here as my guest until I leave, when your duties will start. However, I'll pay you from today, so you won't lose out.'

She shook her head. 'I've been paid——'

'I imagine they'll want some back,' he said drily, 'when you resign, which is something you had better do straight away. I'll contact the Education Board and the head-mistress, and if you'll give me your key I'll get someone to pack up your belongings at the hostel——'

'No, everything's at my mother's,' she said. 'I'll get them——'

He interrupted in his turn. 'Would you like me to contact your mother?'

She shook her head, feeling as though she had been run over by a bulldozer. 'No, I'll write to her, thank you. And you don't have to pay me until I start working for you.'

He looked directly at her, and she realised how he had got to the top. Certainly he had started with all the advantages, but if this was a sample of the way he worked his business associates probably suffered from the feeling that their skins were permanently marked with tyre tracks.

'I set the conditions of employment, Oriel,' he said softly. 'I make the rules.'

Something flinched inside her. 'And I obey them?'

'You do.'

It was said without heat, but the flick of the whip raised weals on her emotions. Stonily she replied, 'Very well, Mr Stephenson.'

'Oho!' he said softly, wicked amusement glinting in his smile. 'My name is Blaize, Oriel. I want Sarah to

feel that she belongs to a family, and she's not going to
feel that way with you pokering up and calling me Mr
Stephenson every time I annoy you.'

She folded her lips firmly, her dismay at being relegated to employee status very real, even though she tried
to tell herself that she had no right to feel so hurt.

'Say it,' he commanded. And when she made no attempt to say his name he went on evenly, 'I decide, Oriel,
not you. Look at me.'

Stubbornly she kept her gaze averted, so that the per-
emptory forefinger under her chin came as a shock.
Quick flags of colour stained her cheeks; her lashes shot
up as she met his steely look. Her mouth dried, for the
determination in his eyes heated into something else, a
glitter of desire, fierce, compelling.

She tried to take a step back, out of the danger zone,
but his hands at her wrists caught her fast. 'I make the
rules—remember?'

His mouth was hard and demanding on her unwilling
lips, unexpectedly cool. Perhaps, she thought, striving
desperately to keep her head, he was only mimicking
desire. Her hands came up and pushed at him, but he
was so strong she didn't have a hope of freeing herself.

Instinct, perhaps self-preservation, ordered her to
remain quiescent. She stood without protest as he held
her against the lean hardness of his body, conscious of
the deliberate plundering of her mouth for his own
sensual gratification.

No one before had ever roused the beast she hadn't
even known was caged deep within her. A tide of sensation so strong that it almost carried her away surged
with unbearable force through her; she thought dazedly
that she had never known the meaning of the word
'fierce' before. This was no shrinking maidenly passion
she felt; it was eager and demanding, responding to the
passion in his kiss with fire and need. She wanted him

with every cell of her body, wanted to feel his imprint on her, in her, wanted to take him and ravish him so that he would never test another woman by kissing her, because to touch another woman would be a betrayal he couldn't contemplate.

For as his mouth gentled, touched the long golden length of her throat and sent tiny tremors through her by nipping on the lobe of her ear, she knew that he was testing her. If she surrendered to his effortless sexual charisma, if she showed him just how easily he could smash down the walls of inhibition around her, then he would know he had a weapon she couldn't fight, and sooner or later it would be wielded.

Was this what had happened to the last governess?

His seeking mouth found the soft hollow below her ear, lingered there with seductive pressure against the fine, silken skin; then he lifted his head and rested his cheek against her forehead.

'If,' he threatened in a slurred voice, 'you call me Mr Stephenson again that's what you can expect—with less restraint each time you do it. Even when you try to freeze me out you have a mouth as sweet as wild honey.'

Oriel drew in a deep breath in a vain attempt to calm her raging nerves. 'If you do,' she stated, shaking, 'contract or no contract, I'll go. You have no right to make me the object of your shop-worn gallantry. It's called sexual harassment, and there are laws against it.'

'I make the laws,' he mocked, releasing her. His mouth was relaxed, all tension gone from his expression, but his eyes still held a warning light as they travelled insolently over her flushed face and parted, bee-stung lips.

'Not those laws,' she flashed angrily. 'I didn't ask to be mauled like a—like a streetwalker!'

He gave her an insolent stare. 'Anything less like a streetwalker would be hard to find. You kiss like a virgin. And you were asking for it, even though the provocation was probably unconscious. But prim or not, you enjoyed it. Oh, you give an excellent imitation of an iceberg, but your mouth softens adorably under mine, and the flush of passion is still staining your skin.'

The silver blade of his gaze rested with cynical enjoyment on her confused face, swept across the pink-flushed silk of her throat.

She rallied, lifting her head with proud resistance. 'I won't be treated like a half-wit, intimidated by kisses, brought into line by your strength and lack of principles. And I'm not available for light relief when you're in between mistresses!'

He laughed and walked across to the desk, where he surveyed her with the cool speculation of the businessman, big and bronze and domineering. 'I haven't heard that word since I gave up reading Georgette Heyer,' he said calmly. 'However, if you need reassurance, I have no intention of using you as a convenience between liaisons. I am not quite so unprincipled as that.'

The lick of contempt in his voice deepened her flush. She muttered, 'All right, I'm sorry, but you must admit you had no right to kiss me.'

'Very well,' he said easily, as though his mind was already on other far more important things, 'I'll admit I shouldn't have given in to temptation, I promise not to do it again—and now will you go, before you provoke me into the sort of reaction we both will regret.'

CHAPTER FIVE

LATER that morning Simon wandered along the beach to the classroom under the pohutukawa tree, whistling the tuneless notes he used as a kind of aural signature.

'Enough for this morning,' Oriel said to her pupil.

Sarah looked longingly at the picture she had been drawing, but gave up without protest when she saw the big launch nose around the headland.

'Mr Howard went in to get some books for me to read,' she said importantly. 'Mrs Howard told me.'

Simon flung himself down on to the grass. In spite of Oriel's insistence that he wear sunscreen his back was already burnt dark by the sun. A slash of bold blue zinc ointment across his nose and cheeks and over his lips gave him a clownish look.

Sarah gurgled. 'You look like a Nindian,' she said.

He gave her a teasing grin and sent another towards Oriel. In ten years' time, she thought, he's going to be falling over women wherever he goes. Young as he was, he had some of Blaize's imperious attraction, the flagrant masculine charm that was so unfairly handed out to the deserving and undeserving alike.

She had felt it that morning. Her cheeks burned as she recalled those unsparing kisses, and her incandescent response. At least she hadn't buckled at the knees; she had emerged with some sort of pride. It had been hard, though. Until then she had never understood how easy it would be to surrender, dragged under by a merciless current of passion and need.

From the grass at her feet Simon made a little exclamation and sat up. 'It's Mr Weatherall,' he said, peering at the launch still halfway across the bay.

Sarah and Oriel squinted into the sun, following the line of his gaze. A dark man of medium height walked along the deck and disappeared into the deckhouse.

'Who's Mr Weatherall?' Oriel asked.

'Uncle Blaize's personal assistant.' Simon grinned and rolled over. 'He's nice, quiet, but he can play a neat game of squash and cricket.'

Having failed lamentably to show any signs of interest in either, Oriel was already familiar with Simon's worship of both sports. She said amiably, 'So he could steal ice-creams from little children and kick cats as a hobby, but he'd still be a nice man.'

'Yeah,' Simon breathed cheekily. 'Much nicer than dumb-bells who don't know the difference between a squash racket and a cricket bat.'

She laughed. 'I do so. If the man carrying it wears long white trousers it's a cricket bat. If he wears shorts it's a squash racket.'

Simon hooted and got to his feet as she began to pick up the paper and pencils they had been using. 'Come on, Sarah,' she said cheerfully, 'let's tidy up.'

'Can I go with Simon to meet the boat?'

She nodded. 'After we tidy up.'

'You'll be lucky,' Simon teased. 'Sarah never tidies up after herself.'

'Do so!'

'Nah, you don't.'

The cheerful bickering continued while Sarah piled everything more or less neatly in the centre of the table, then looked up at Oriel, who chuckled. 'Yes,' she said with resignation, 'that will do.'

She held out her hand. Sarah looked surprised but took it happily enough, her warm, slightly sticky fingers nestling confidingly in Oriel's. Had her previous governess ignored the child's need for affectionate physical contact?

'Mr Weatherall' was a handsome man but strangely inconspicuous, as though he had spent all his life trying to fade into the background. Perhaps that was what working for Blaize did for people! However, he had a charming smile, one that came spontaneously when Oriel said, 'Mr Weatherall, I presume?'

'No, no,' he said, holding out his hand. 'That's my line. Miss Oriel Radford, I presume?'

She shook hands, thinking wryly, So Blaize has contacted him about me. I wonder why. Then, with a flash of intuition, So that he could check me out, of course.

Well, naturally. He wasn't to know that she was the person she said she was. Blaize had probably been the target for all sorts of people, women as well as men, ever since he was as tall as Simon.

Thank heavens I'm not rich! she thought fervently.

A smile pinned to her face, she walked along the sun-warmed planks of the jetty, listening to the muted screech of the wheels on the trolley as Simon helped Kathy's husband push it along. It was piled with boxes and bags, much, no doubt, of the food for the party in three days' time.

Sarah clung to her hand, telling Blaize's assistant about the changes in her life. Oriel liked the way he listened and spoke to the child, as though she were a responsible adult. Constantly devalued herself by a mother who didn't understand her, Oriel was acutely conscious of the same attitude in others. It made her prickly and antagonistic, but in this case there was no need. Mr Weatherall liked Sarah, and it showed.

'...and Oriel's not limping much today,' Sarah wound down. 'Her foot's all funny colours under the bandages, but she told Uncle Blaize it doesn't hurt much when he asked her this morning. I saw it when she was getting up.'

'I'm glad you're recovering quickly,' James Weatherall said, his limpid eyes giving no hint of his enjoyment of Sarah's artless recital. 'That was quite an experience you had. The last part of it must have been agonising.'

She shrugged. 'Oh, it hurt, but I used a stick, and when it got too much I crawled. I was lucky, it could have been a lot worse. Someone had to do it—my cousin had a broken leg.'

His shrewd gaze softened. 'Yes, so I understand. I'm glad to see you looking so well.' His eyes moved from her face and his expression altered, not much, but enough to catch Oriel's attention. She too looked ahead and saw Blaize standing, somehow ominously still, in the shade on the terrace, watching them.

He smiled as they came up, but there was no warmth in it. A tiny shard of ice slithered across her spine.

'I see you two have introduced yourselves,' was all he said. 'James, come to the office with me, will you? There are a few things I want to get done right away.'

James Weatherall's arrival coincided with two days of rain and the threat of yet another tropical storm. He and Blaize spent most of the time sequestered in the office, leaving Oriel to look after two children who found the constant soft drizzle and the heat extremely trying. Sarah was all right while she was doing her lessons, her determination to succeed preventing any thought of giving up, but after she had completed several jigsaws and all the wet-weather activities Oriel could dream up, she became petulant and began to quarrel with her brother.

He too was at a loose end, the manager's children having gone to Auckland to visit some cousins. Banned from the kitchen after he had demolished a cold roast chicken Kathy had had other plans for, he mooched around gloomily. Not even television was of any use; the only thing he wanted to watch was the test cricket series, and that was rained out.

On the afternoon of the second day Oriel found both children bickering in real earnest, exchanging insults with a fervour that threatened to degenerate into a brawl. Firmly she said, 'Right, that's enough. We're going swimming.'

Both stared at her, then Sarah pointed out, 'It's raining.'

'So it is. So it won't matter if we get wet, will it?' Simon's voice was scornful, but he looked pleased at the prospect.

Oriel flashed him a stern, minatory look. 'It's very warm—far too hot, in fact, and we all need the exercise.'

Grinning, they decided that, strange as it seemed, it had the makings of a good idea. Ten minutes later they met in the gazebo. Huddled into her towel, Sarah was pouting, but when she saw both Oriel and Simon drop their wraps and set off for the beach with identical expressions of anticipation, curiosity drove her to follow. Oriel had taken the bandage off her foot that morning, and although the bruises were not a pretty sight, turning yellow and purple, the resultant freedom was worth it. She was now limping much less, although the wretched thing still swelled by the end of each day. Apparently the doctor's forecast of at least a month before it was as good as ever was going to be correct.

Flattened by the gentle persistence of the rain, the sea was lukewarm, tiny waves running silently up the wet sand. Just as they reached the edge the rain eased and died, although a heavy mist was almost as wetting. The atmosphere was distinctly eerie, the house a dark, formless bulk, the beach a pale half-moon coming from and fading into mist with pohutukawa trees looming weirdly along it, the jetty a skeletal edifice where the water smoothed with oily languor between the piles.

'No fooling,' Oriel commanded in the sort of voice that no one could misunderstand. 'And no diving. It would be far too easy to lose yourself in this.'

Awed by the steamy, mysterious ambience, both children stayed close by, speaking in low voices that were oddly muffled by the mist.

Simon said suddenly, 'I feel as though a dinosaur might rise up out of the water beside us.'

Sarah gave a little squeak and looked around. 'Oh, look, there's its eye!' she hissed, pointing to the diffused golden glow of a window in the house.

'That's the office.' Simon rolled over on to his back, seeing how long he could stay floating without moving anything. 'Gosh, Uncle Blaize and Mr Weatherall have been busy! Perhaps they're going to take someone over.'

Sarah trod water, her small paws dog-paddling slowly. 'Are you going to work for Uncle Blaize when you grow up?'

Simon said magnificently, 'Never. I'm going to be a professional cricketer, like Hadlee or Crowe.'

Given his passion for sport, this was a not unexpected answer. Oriel grinned. 'What are you going to do?' she asked Sarah.

'I'm going to be a deep-sea diver. I can dive really well now—Uncle Blaize taught me.'

Oriel kissed the wet, earnest little face. 'A great idea!'

Her charge gave a pleased little wriggle. 'And I'm going to work on an oil rig and find pirates' treasure.'

'Good for you!'

Simon said, 'The dinosaur's closed its eyes. It's gone to sleep.'

At Sarah's shiver Oriel said briskly, 'Come on, time to go in.'

For once, neither objected. As they neared the little summerhouse a tall figure loomed up out of the mist.

Oriel's heart gave a sudden leap, but Sarah squealed, 'Uncle Blaize, I thought you were a dinosaur!' as she ran towards him.

He fended her off expertly. 'Really? I have a long neck and scales?'

Giggling, Sarah shouted, 'No, you've got big teeth and a yellow eye!' and raced past him, running soundlessly across the wet grass after her brother.

Oriel started to follow them, but an imperative hand on her arm stopped her flight.

'I like that bathing-suit,' he said, and leaned forward and pulled the zip down an inch. 'Have you missed me these last few days?' he asked softly, his knuckles brushing the cool satin swell of her breast.

She jerked away. Fingers made clumsy by cold fumbled with the recalcitrant zip until she managed to haul it right up again.

'No,' she said icily, tensing as his glance travelled the entire length of her body, lingering, openly following the artful line of the black panel from the slight swell of her breasts to where it disappeared at the juncture of her thighs, admiring the smooth, wet length of her legs, then starting back again.

It was a deliberate attack on her self-possession, an intrusion of the most blatant sort, and she was angry, her eyes a searing, smoking blue.

'I like it very much,' he said, his voice modulated by the thick blanket of mist so that they seemed to be cocooned in an intimate prison. 'But I think perhaps you had better get another one. Simon is at an impressionable age——'

'That's sick,' she said flatly. 'Simon is a child.'

'Really?' He lifted his brows at her. 'I can remember what it was like being fourteen—all those hormones surging around with no outlet. And James is impressionable too.'

Anyone less impressionable than the poker-faced personal assistant it would be hard to find. 'I've never heard such nasty rubbish,' she said scornfully.

'But then you haven't had much to do with men, or their inconvenient urges, have you?'

His eyes were on her breasts, and to her astonishment she felt a tingling, drawing sensation there, at once painful and exciting. Shame and embarrassment held her in a rigid grip.

'How our bodies betray us,' he said softly, lifting his eyes so that she could see the lick of flame heating the grey to a molten silver. 'Infuriating, isn't it? Behind us there are centuries of civilisation, of custom and restraint, of conditioning, and yet the basic urges lie in wait, needing only one of a multitude of tiny physical signs, and it all goes for nothing. You are young and very nicely packaged and female, I am a male whose hormones are still in production, and so we want to lie down together and make a baby. Because that's what it's for, Oriel, the complete sequence of romance and love, tinsel and lies and long, sizzling looks across the room. Just so that we can pass our genes on to the next generation. Poets have written immortal lines about it, romantics have died for it, and the whole thing is nature's joke on a species that takes itself too seriously.'

She shivered, her eyes imprisoned by the stormy dazzle of his, all her secret fervours sabotaged by the complete cynicism in his words.

'There's some excuse for you,' he said quietly. 'You're young. But I've seen too much of it, I know how it works. And I'm not going to allow long, sleek limbs and a sweetly provocative smile, and eyes that turn smoky when they look at me, to send me off down that road.'

'I don't—they don't——' Her voice cracked, unable to articulate the thoughts that whirled around her brain.

'Yes, you do. I do. We do.' His hands shot out, grabbed her and pulled her into the warmth of his body. His lips came to rest on her forehead. Against the soft, damp skin he said harshly, 'I can feel your heart beating like a caged thing. So is mine, Oriel, and for the same reason.'

Something harsh and hot blocked her throat, but she swallowed it down and said with fierce determination, 'I don't want—I am not going to enter into any sort of relationship with you.'

'I know that,' he said coolly, kissing her eyelids closed. 'You want marriage, all nice and legal, with a lifetime contract, your body as security.'

The stinging contempt in his voice wrenched her from the languor that paralysed her. She tried to swing free, but his grip tightened. Bemused, she lifted her lashes to meet eyes that held devil's fire. As his face came closer she tried to bite him, but his mouth crushed hers into silence and stillness, forcing her lips apart so that he could make himself master of the sweet, hidden depths. Speared by a pang of sensation, her body jerked, and a low, muffled little sound died stillborn in her throat. The hands that had been pushing him away tightened into fists on his shirt; she shuddered, and he lifted his head for a moment and whispered something, then bent again and gentled her mouth into returning his kiss.

It was shattering. Heat that sprang into life in the pit of her stomach became transmuted to a fiery need. She pressed against him, taking an angry delight in the hard masculinity of his body, hers throbbing, aching, pierced by hunger.

Her mouth shaped to his, taking and giving, glorying in the different textures, the different tastes. She thought she might die with desire, her whole being ravished by this intolerable delight, this feeling of urgency and need.

'Oh, hell,' he said against her lips. 'Your mouth is like crushed silk, warm and throbbing. It's like kissing a flower. And your eyes... How did you reach twenty-three without losing your innocence when you've got eyes that promise all the delights of paradise, dark pleasures, secret, decadent sins that enslave a man, netting him in a cage of ecstasy until he's drowned in it...?'

Racked by fever, she gasped when his hands slid down to her hips and pulled her into the hard cradle of his, her softness shocking against his hardness. Groaning, sighing, she rocked against him, so lost in the bewildering pleasure that she didn't even realise he had pulled the zip right down until he kissed the throbbing flesh he had exposed, his mouth lingering with a magician's enchantment over the slight curves.

The desperate hunger intensified into shimmering sensation, ravishing, ecstatic. She had never known that a man's mouth could summon rapture so easily. The friendly mist swirled around, shielding them in swathes of drapery, cool on her skin, a tactile contrast to the heat of their bodies, the fire of his mouth on her breasts.

Simon's voice echoed eerily. 'Oriel? Oriel, where are you?'

She felt as though the world had crashed down on to her. Rigid with shock and shame, she lurched away from Blaize, only dimly realising that he had begun to set her free before she had heard the boy's voice.

'I won't be a moment,' she said. Her voice sounded surprisingly steady, but she drew a deep, quivering breath and turned blindly away.

'OK.' Simon's voice faded; he was going back to the house.

She grabbed her towel and ran back in as though all the devils in hell were after her.

That night, safe at last in her bedroom, she looked at her arms and mouth with disgust. There were bruises on her skin, faint but obvious if you knew where to look, and her mouth had the ripe contours that denoted thorough kissing.

Dragging the brush through her hair, she watched with unseeing eyes as the curls sprang into place. She hadn't seen Blaize after that; he and James had shared dinner in the office, and she had eaten with the children, going up early to bed in a blue terror that he might emerge and she would have to face him.

Only to find that she had to face herself.

Hiding in her room, she could remember the exact inflexions of his voice, the movement of his beautiful mouth as he had spoken, the cold cynicism of each word. And every one of the heated, frantic moments she had spent in his arms, her moral standards banished into some hazy limbo while she let him do exactly what he wanted to do with the body he despised himself for wanting.

But not as much as she despised herself. She had melted—no, she had not *melted*, she had become aggressive and demanding, pressing herself against him like some wanton, shamelessly inciting him to take her, her mouth clinging to his in a duel that was heading in only one direction.

'Oh, God,' she whispered, turning the light off so she could no longer be tormented by the memories burning in her eyes. 'What am I going to do?'

Her first instinct was to flee back to the safety of the life she had known previously, but of course she couldn't, she had signed that contract. The next three months stretched out like eternity. Her heart ached at the damage she was going to wreak on Sarah, but self-preservation made only one course possible. She couldn't stay, not after this afternoon. Ruthlessly she banished the memory of the promise she had made to the child.

But when she had left, what was she going to do? She would have to start looking around for another job, trying to rebuild a life Blaize had shattered with one touch of his practised hands, one experienced kiss.

At least Simon had blundered upon them in time. What else might she have done in the turmoil of her first experience of overwhelming passion? Begged him to take her? She writhed in shame, because she might just have done that.

Never again! she thought in horror. If that was what desire did to you she was never going to allow it into her life. Better to die without experiencing fulfilment if to achieve it she had to surrender to that mindless need.

She had never realised how important it was for her to remain in command of her life, and the heady, wild excitement she felt with Blaize was far too volatile for control. In his arms she became witless, a slave to sensation and the hunger for an unknowable more, and she could not, dared not be captured again by that dark enchantment.

Sane again, with the bitter taste of humiliation in her mouth, she realised how close she had come to throwing away all her self-respect on a man who couldn't have made it more obvious that the only thing he felt for her was lust. Not that she could blame him for that. It was all she felt for him. She wasn't in love with him. Just nature's little joke, she thought bleakly. A joke on her.

At least there would be no repetition. The self-contempt she had heard in his voice, seen in his face, would ensure that.

Towards dawn she fell asleep, to wake with a throbbing head and heavy eyes to a day where the sun shone serenely in a calm sky. Perversely, the resumption of fine weather intensified her misery. For long moments she stood in the window, watching the sheep move quietly across the green hillsides, listening to the persistent shrill call of hundreds of cicadas in the trees.

From somewhere below Kathy called out something, then laughed. Today was the day of the party, the social event of the year at Pukekaroro.

Today was the first day of purgatory for Oriel Radford, who was a fool.

Blaize was in the morning-room, the sun striking a warm amber halo from his head as he drank coffee and teased his niece. Simon and James Weatherall were deep in conversation; cricket, no doubt. They all stood as she limped into the room. Antiquated manners, she thought, smiling with determined impartiality around the room, but for these men, it was second nature. As was Blaize's automatic service of holding her chair for her.

'Thank you,' she murmured as she flicked out her napkin.

Unconscious of any undercurrents, Sarah told her exuberantly, 'Oriel, Uncle Blaize says we have to stay out of Kathy's way today, so he's taking us out in the boat. He and Mr Weatherall have done so much work when it was raining they can have today off! But Mr Weatherall isn't coming with us, he's going to walk up to the dam and paint a picture. And he bought a new thing for my tummy, it's just a band that you put round your arm, and then you're not sick at all. So I don't have to take a pill!'

'Lovely.' Oriel gave her an uncomplicated smile. With an effort she transferred it to Blaize, meeting his eyes for a fraction of a second. 'You won't be needing me, so I'll help Kathy.'

'Of course I need you,' he returned, his smile sharp and ironic. 'I can't look after Sarah by myself. She wears me out.'

While Sarah giggled and made a face, Oriel's precarious equilibrium tilted. 'I'll be of more use——' she began, but was interrupted with smooth finality.

'You'll be of most use with us,' Blaize said. 'Eat your breakfast, and then you can check the lunch with Kathy. She may have forgotten just how much Simon can eat.'

Simon hotly denied the imputation of greed, but had to subside at the mention of the roast chicken he had poached from the refrigerator.

An hour later they were all on board, with Simon and Sarah insisting on showing Oriel the controls; she was interested to learn that Sarah knew as much about their function as her brother, and pleased, because it reinforced her belief that the child was extremely intelligent.

Simon said importantly, 'This is the helm indicator. It's necessary because with an outdrive and hydraulic steering you have to know which way the propeller is pointing when you put her in gear.'

Oriel didn't ask why. She stared at the multitude of dials, composing her face into an expression of great interest while Sarah showed her the depth-finder and the radar.

From behind came Blaize's ironic voice. 'You're dazzling her with your brilliance, you two. Simon, would you like to take the boat out?'

It appeared that above all things Simon would like to. His face lit up with delight and he stammered, 'Would I ever! I can do it.'

Blaize turned to Oriel, pinning her with his cool, questioning glance. 'Welcome aboard. How do you like her?'

'Very much.' Resentment iced her words. 'No expense has been spared to make her wonderful, so of course I like her. Is she only used when you're here?'

Simon said cheerfully, 'No, people who come to stay here use her a lot too, don't they, Uncle Blaize? And Uncle Blaize charters her out the rest of the time.'

'Of course.' He was all taut charm, meeting the challenge she had been unaware of making with mockery and malice. 'I'm a businessman, remember? Which reminds me, Oriel, I looked over the contract this morning.'

Tantalisingly he waited for her to answer.

'Yes?'

'Quite watertight,' he said without emphasis, only the quick, splintering glance from his half-closed eyes revealing the taunt.

Devil! He must have known that she had spent a good portion of the night wondering whether he had any right to tie her down to a contract like that. He was making it obvious where she fitted into his life. An employee, bound by contracts. Oh, no doubt he would take her if she offered herself, accept all that she had to give, and tell himself that she had no right to complain at the little he was willing to give her back, because he had warned her how he felt.

It did not seem possible that less than twenty-four hours before she had lain against him, made temporarily insane by the urgent demands of her body for release, a slave to his tenderness and passion and her own.

Pride held her head high. 'I hadn't thought it might be anything other than watertight,' she said, smiling resolutely up at him. 'I'm under no illusions as to your expertise in all things, including the drafting of contracts.'

Her voice lingered delicately over the word expertise, investing it with unmistakable meaning.

But if her shot went home he did not reveal it. Looking bored, he murmured, 'Thank you. Simon, are you ready to go?'

It seemed to Oriel that the fewer people watching him the more composed Simon might be, so she made her way down the short companionway to the main cabin and spent the next five minutes stowing into the refrigerator the enormous amount of food that Kathy had thought necessary. After a quick glance had reassured her that they were safely out in the bay she went back on deck, to discover that Simon and Sarah were up on the flying bridge with Blaize.

One glance at the ladder and she realised that she wasn't going to be able to get up there without putting quite a bit of strain on her foot. Blaize looked down, saw her worried look, and came lithely down, his lean, heavily muscled legs dark against the pristine paintwork of the boat.

Something primitive and anticipatory moved in the pit of Oriel's stomach. She stood with closed face, willing herself not to betray the fact that she wanted him.

'Don't attempt those steps,' he commanded as he came up to her. 'I'll look after Sarah while she's up there.'

She nodded and turned away, but almost immediately her name whipped her head around. He was looking at her with something of the same hunger that gnawed at her, his face oddly bleak, the stark bone structure revealed in the uncompromising strength of the sun. In that moment she realised that he could wound her for life, that what she felt was so much more than simple lust.

She was perilously close to falling in love with him. If he knew, would he send her away—or would he take advantage of the fact? Was he brutal enough to use her hopeless attraction to keep her as Sarah's substitute mother until Sarah no longer needed her?

Most desperately she wanted to believe that he was too honourable, but cold logic forced her to accept that he was a complex man, one she didn't really understand.

What she did know was that he loved his niece. And he was hard enough to hold her to a contract when he knew that she wanted to go.

She would have to strive to overcome her infatuation before she fell so fathoms deep that she became addicted to him, the sight and sound of him, pathetically grateful for any little crumbs of attention he might give her.

Fixing a bright, meaningless smile on her face, she said, 'Yes?'

'Don't look so tragic,' he said, watching her with eyes as opaque as burnished metal. 'Things will work out. They always do.'

Nodding, she turned away; she knew when he left her by the way the hairs on the back of her neck eased down.

The wind tugged at her, teasing her locks into tendrils of tightly wound black silk around her face. She licked lips suddenly dry, tasting the faint film of salt. Out here on the water it was cooler, a little less humid than on shore, and she was grateful for the refuge from the prickly, enervating weather of the past few days.

It must be Saturday, she thought tiredly, watching a fleet of yachts racing, their jujube-coloured sails graceful and fragile on the brilliant blue water. Odd how she had lost count of the days and the weeks, content to live in a timeless enchantment. At least, that was how it had seemed until yesterday. Wincing, she dragged her mind away from the one subject it seemed unable to avoid, like a tongue exploring a broken tooth.

Rain had worked its familiar magic on the summer coast. Hills, usually toast-coloured by now, were a dozen shades of green blending into the elusive blue-violet of the bush-covered range in the distance. Towards Kerikeri a sombre forest of pine trees, living expression of faith in the future, marched over the last tiny volcano to erupt in the district two thousand years ago. Gulls swooped and wheeled above the boat, glittering silver in a moment of glory in the sun's rays. Faster and sleeker, flocks of graceful terns dived to capture the smaller fish driven by fleet, wandering shoals of kahawai.

The deep throb of the engines altered, slowed. Footsteps on the companionway brought Oriel's head around. Blaize was swinging down the steps, Sarah trailing behind him with the expression of one who was acting under strong sufferance.

His hair ruffled by the wind, Blaize looked, Oriel thought painfully, young and devil-may-care, almost recklessly handsome. It couldn't be more obvious that he was not suffering any of the anguish that racked her.

Once down he got busy with lines and lures, telling her, 'We're going to troll for kahawai. Simon can't resist catching fish.'

'It's not very good eating, is it?' How calm her voice sounded, level, almost dispassionate!

'Spoken like all true New Zealanders, who consider snapper the only fish worth eating.'

'Oh, come on, now,' she protested, catching Sarah as she jumped into her arms. 'I like hapuka and gurnard, mullet and flounder—even eel!'

He looked across at her, laughter dancing in his eyes. 'Very well, then, I acquit you of being a true New Zealander. Kahawai is a delicious eating-fish. If we catch any I'll get Kathy to show you how to cook it.'

'*I* like it,' Sarah announced. 'Can I help, Uncle Blaize?'

'Certainly, treasure, I could do with a little help.'

Oriel watched. He was patient with the child's occasional clumsiness, and his affection softened and gentled his voice and manner. He was an excellent uncle; he would be just as good a father.

The thought of bearing a child for him made her bones go to water.

CHAPTER SIX

IT WAS then that Oriel realised that, far from being on the verge of falling in love, she had already passed over the invisible boundary and was fathoms deep.

'You fool!' she half whispered. 'Oh, you fool!'

How many other women had gazed at Blaize with exactly the same lovesick regard, trying to imprint on their minds and hearts the physical reality of him, the dominant angles of face and jaw, the stark, masculine lines of shoulder and arm, the lithe frame, the hidden excitement of lean hips and strong thighs, the potent, blazing maleness that sent out an overt message of fulfilment to every female in sight?

And how many had taken that further terrifying step into love? How had it happened? She could not pinpoint a time or a place. Perhaps it had been his gentleness with his little niece that had triggered it; perhaps it had been inevitable from the beginning, when she had been hurt and exhausted and unable to cope, and he had been so kind, so protective.

What was love, after all? Surely not the cosmic joke he thought it, the genetic urge to perpetuate the species?

If it were that, she would feel the same about any kind, sexually attractive man. Mentally she reviewed those she knew, frowning as she realised that she was mentally and emotionally repulsed by the thought of making love to any of them.

But oh, what a fool she was to let down her guard and fall in love with a man who was a complete and total cynic!

Perhaps it was calf-love, an adolescent crush that was fierce and painful but soon over. Never forgotten, but recalled with sympathetic amusement as well as affection.

She had had crushes in her adolescence, hormone-based, unfulfilled, for none of the boys she had been attracted to had been in the least interested in the tall, skinny teenager she had been then.

And no one, least of all Blaize Stephenson, who could have any woman he wanted, would be interested in the tall, thin woman she had become, small-breasted and snake-hipped, with the ballet lessons her mother had insisted she take the only thing between her and that adolescent awkwardness.

Not for the first time Oriel thought of her small, dainty mother, and the men she seemed to attract without even trying. What was it that gave some women that power?

Or some men, she thought, her eyes moving with delicate greed over the downbent bronze head and the lean fingers fixing lures to the line. The subliminal message that a man would be excellent in bed? An excellent provider? If he was right, and love was merely a fiction to make the propagation of genes pleasurable, then a man who had that air of security, of calm, strong competence, would certainly be attractive to women. After all, the fate of children rested upon those qualities.

But even as the thoughts raced through her brain, she knew it was not that alone which made Blaize so attractive. She had not fallen in love with him for his competence, or the masculine charisma he wore so effortlessly. Simply, inevitably, fatally, she had recognised him as her other half, the one man she needed.

Colour burned across her cheeks as she dragged her eyes away. She had to go; she was not built to cope with pain on this scale, and if she stayed pain would be the inevitable result. How would she feel when he began to see one of the beautiful women his name had been connected with? Bloody furious, she thought, hating the ferocious surge of jealousy that tightened every muscle in her body.

Trying to banish the thoughts that roiled murkily around in her mind, she asked, 'Do you need any help?'

'No, Sarah and I are the experts. All we require of you is that you appreciate the ones we catch and confirm the size of the ones that got away.' Blaize got to his feet and called out to Simon, 'OK, let her go!'

The engines deepened, the boat surged up and forward, ploughing a straight furrow through the sea, and Blaize and Sarah began to pay out the lines over the stern.

A few seconds later a triumphant yell from Sarah revealed a strike; almost immediately Blaize called out, and Simon cut the engines. He leaned over the flying bridge and called down, 'Let's have another go!'

'No, we don't need any more.'

'Oh, Uncle *Blaize*!'

He looked up, laughing but uncompromising. 'Bloodthirsty young larrikin! Any more would be a waste, and you know it.'

Watched with ghoulish interest by Sarah, he cleaned and scaled the fish on the neat little platform at the stern provided for just that task, then handed them over to Oriel, asking blandly, 'Put them in the fridge, will you?'

When she came back he had washed his hands and was smiling down at a well-satisfied Sarah. Oriel's heart jumped, rather, she thought hollowly, like the leap of a doomed fish when it struck the lure, and when he transferred the smile to her she went under without any hope of recovery.

'What better life could there be?' he asked. 'A day on a summer coast, the sea, food we've caught ourselves, and a family to share it all with?'

Hugging his hand to her cheek, Sarah smiled, her small face incandescent with delight. Oriel envied her, and at the same time realised that he was deadly serious. Something impelled her to say shrewdly, 'Lovely, but not as a regular thing.'

'Why?'

A prickle of some unknown emotion ran between her shoulders, but she said brightly, 'You need a challenge.'

He lifted his brows. 'Go on,' he invited softly.

She was speaking out of turn, but she went on just the same. 'This is serenity. It's wonderful, but not for a regular thing. I'm sure there's enough in the kitty to make every day like this for you if you wanted it to be, but you choose to work. Why?'

'Upbringing? My parents believed firmly that everyone owed the world something for being born.'

'And you agree with them. Besides, you like a challenge. You didn't really enjoy catching those fish, did you?'

Sarah looked up at him. He glanced down at her worshipful face before saying briskly, 'I'll agree that I prefer a battle. Trolling for kahawai is not as much fun as catching them on a light line. They're one of the best fighting fish in the sea. Once you've caught one like that you know you've won a battle.'

Oriel nodded, and he added, 'Stop looking so smug! I'll admit I enjoy a challenge. And that,' he said softly, 'should make you wary, Miss Psychologist.'

Her astonishment showed in her face. 'What on earth do you mean?'

That familiar and hateful mockery was back in the polished eyes. 'Think about it,' he advised.

Sarah stirred, looking from one to the other, apparently aware of the fine threads of tension spun out of the conversation. 'Can I go up on the flying bridge?' she asked tentatively.

'Of course you can.' He boosted her up the steps. Over his shoulder he finished, 'We'll be landing on one of the islands for lunch in half an hour or so.'

The island they chose was popular, with other boats in most of the bays, so Blaize took them around until they found a tiny beige crescent that was empty, a smooth melon slice of sand with great pohutukawas creating pockets of dense shade and coolness. When the muted roar of the powerful engines died away, the shrill violins of the cicadas rose in a throbbing crescendo, the sound of summer.

Oriel had repacked the food along with plates and cutlery and a blackened kettle, which was obviously a survivor of similar picnics, and organised sun-hats and screen and insect repellant as well as bathing-suits. Blaize stacked both provisions and people into the inflatable dinghy and he and Simon rowed them ashore.

'You have to row in,' Sarah told Oriel seriously, 'it's not a picnic if you put the engine in the dinghy. You might frighten the pirates.'

Oriel grinned. 'Fair enough. But were there pirates in New Zealand?'

'Oh, yes, Bully Hayes was a pirate, nearly. Some of his desc—grandchildren still live around here, you know. Up north.'

'I can see I'll have to brush up on my history,' Oriel mused. 'How about treasure?'

'Well, in Whangaroa harbour there's the treasure of the *Boyd*. No one's ever found that.'

'No one knows if there was a treasure,' Simon interpolated.

'Of course there was!' His sister was indignant. She was also a realist, as she proved by continuing, 'No one can prove there wasn't, anyway. I don't care, I like to think there was.'

Oriel dragged her eyes away from the smooth power of Blaize's movements, and said comfortingly, 'Of course there was. And if there wasn't, we can imagine our own. Black pearls from Tahiti and Fala'isi.'

'Sandalwood and gold from Fiji.' That was Blaize.

Simon chipped in. 'Opals and diamonds from Australia.'

Sarah laughed excitedly. 'And beautiful greenstone from New Zealand!'

'Where do you think they buried it?' Simon entered into the spirit of the thing with gusto. 'They'd be intending to come back for it, so they'd mark it with sightings that needn't be permanent.'

Sarah scanned the tiny bay, her eyes narrowed as she rejected various sites. Finally, just as the dinghy crunched on to the sand, she pointed with a dramatic finger at a large rock on one side. 'They'd use that,' she said. 'It's the easiest thing to see here.'

Simon shipped his oars. 'Yep, they probably would. Come on, let's——'

'Just a moment.' Blaize's voice was amused but firm. 'You have work to do. Oriel got all this ready without your help, so you can carry it up, both of you, while I work out where we make a campfire. Then we'll need wood.'

Without demur both children gave up any idea of pursuing the game just then. They helped Oriel carry the cool-box and the equipment up into the shade of one of the sheltering trees, then suggested sites for a campfire, taking into account wind and tide. When that decision was made Simon arranged some stones to contain the fire, and Sarah and Oriel went gathering driftwood from a tiny cove around the headland. It had been scoured clean of sand by the tide, so they had to walk gingerly over the wave-worn stones to collect bleached, salty, sea-burnished twigs and branches.

It was profoundly satisfying. Revelling in the caress of the sun on her shoulders and legs, Oriel searched diligently, occasionally stopping at Sarah's behest to admire a particularly beautiful pebble. She should have been appalled at the predicament she was in, but the perfect weather and the simple, satisfying task and the pleasure of being a part of this family unit, with the man she loved, lifted her spirits so that they showed in the glow in her smoky eyes and a smile that trembled brilliantly on lips suddenly soft and tender.

A yell from behind turned them. Simon and Blaize came towards them, with identical frowns.

Blaize said crisply, 'You shouldn't be hobbling over this uneven surface, Oriel. Go back.'

'Oh, dear,' she sighed. 'Relegated to the boring womanly things.'

He gave her a teasing, not entirely humorous smile. 'Never mind—when your foot is better I'll let you do anything you want,' he promised. A note of lazy sensuality threaded smooth as silk, hot as flame, through his voice.

Without a word she walked back to the picnic area, berating herself for her susceptibility to a pair of grey eyes, and a flexible, deep voice, a smile that was like a blade in her heart.

By the time they returned with armfuls of wood she had regained some of her composure, but it sat uneasily on her so that it only needed a smile, the touch of his hand on hers as she handed him kindling, the subtle yet overpowering tug of her senses, to overset it.

The fire burned, hot but oddly pale in the sunlight, and while water boiled in the blackened billy they ate a superb lunch—roast chicken pieces, a magnificent veal and ham pie into which Simon made great inroads, a pasta salad that was Sarah's favourite, as well as lettuce and tomatoes and avocados, and a jar of Kathy's secret French dressing.

'You're not eating much,' Simon observed, frowning at Oriel. 'Here, have a piece of this pie. It's delicious.'

'I'm sure it is. Thank you.'

Sarah said earnestly, 'Sea air's supposed to make you hungry. Mummy used to say——' Her voice wobbled, but she ploughed on valiantly, 'Mummy used to say she could eat a horse out in the boat, didn't she, Simon?'

'Yeah.' His voice was muffled as he stowed away some more pie, but Oriel saw the pain darkening his eyes.

She said calmly, 'Your mother was quite right, but I haven't got much of an appetite. That's why I'm so thin.'

Simon's jaw dropped. 'You're not thin,' he said, grief forgotten. He turned to his uncle, appealing to the expert. 'Oriel's not skinny, is she? She looks like the models in those awful fashion magazines some girls read all the time. I'll bet if you put all that gunk on your face you'd look just like them, Oriel. Kind of leggy, and—well, kind of pretty.'

Oriel said in a voice she only just managed to keep steady, 'That's the nicest thing I've ever had said to me, Simon.'

'True, too,' Blaize said, enjoying both his nephew's confusion and Oriel's attempts to carry the situation off with *savoir-faire*. He smiled provokingly at her, laughter gleaming slyly in his eyes. 'I couldn't have said it better myself.'

And he took advantage of Simon's innocent compliment to run his eyes down Oriel's body from her high, heated cheekbones to her curling toes, lingering a second on the small upthrusts of her breasts against her shirt, to follow the length of her legs, tanned and smooth and long even when she was sitting with her arms around her knees.

'Very leggy,' he murmured, 'but I don't think pretty is the exact word, Sim. Striking—unforgettable, perhaps. Those eyes are definitely exotic, with their sulky, heavy lids, and such a fascinating shade of blue. And that wild hair seems to have a life of its own, especially when it's salty, as it is now.'

'Still,' Simon said doggedly, 'I reckon she'd do in those magazines, don't you?'

'Oh, I'm sure she would.'

Ignoring the curls of colour along her cheekbones, Oriel returned woodenly, 'You're wrong, I'm afraid. My mother works for one of those model agencies, and she'd have known if I had any potential.'

'Sometimes parents are strangely blind when it comes to their children,' Blaize suggested.

She lifted her head and challenged him. 'Not my mother. She's very astute. She'd have adored a model daughter, and she tried hard to get me up to scratch. She insisted on ballet and gymnastics, had me taught elocution, the piano, drama—you name it, I suffered through it!'

To no avail, her tone implied. Blaize's lashes hid any emotion in his eyes but his voice held only idle curiosity as he asked, 'Did you enjoy any of the lessons?'

'Some.' She put her chin down on to her knees to avoid that too-perceptive gaze and said quietly, 'I loved fencing. I had a friend who used to fence, and I wanted more than anything to do that. But Mother felt it was unfeminine—riding too.' She grimaced. 'Riding gives you big thighs, and swimming masculine shoulders. Not what a young girl needs.'

'Did you try to persuade her to change her mind?'

'I did, but she had strong views. It wasn't worth it.'

'You could,' he pointed out, 'have done some of them after you left home.'

She lifted her shoulders. 'The fact that I didn't probably means that she was right when she said the only reason I wanted to do them was to be contrary.'

'What's contrary?' Sarah's little voice impinged. With a shock Oriel realised that they had an audience.

Smiling, she explained what contrary meant, and after that it was time for the billy tea, which she drank gratefully, enjoying the distinctive, strong yet pleasant taste. Then they tidied up, the children gleefully pouring buckets of water over the ashes. After that Blaize took them for a walk.

With half-closed eyes Oriel watched them disappear into the cicada-shrill depths of the trees, pretending that they were her family, then told herself firmly not to be an idiot and lay on her stomach and dozed. She must have slept properly, because she woke with some alarm at the sound of their voices, suddenly louder as they came out from beneath the trees on to the sand.

'All right,' Blaize agreed. 'For half an hour. Then we'll have a swim, and then, pirates, we'll have to go back home.'

She had been woken from the middle of an erotic dream, one that made her face flush guiltily; she didn't move, hoping he would go with the children. However, she felt his silent approach across the sand with every cell in her body, every tiny hair in her skin lifting in primitive reaction.

Concentrating hard on keeping her breathing regular, she lay still, her back turned to him. For long, prickly moments she knew he stood there, watching her. His gaze on her back, on her legs, on the back of her neck, was like the searing breath of a forest fire. She stiffened at the soft sounds that denoted he was sitting down. The rug gave as he came down. Too close... A shiver ran down her spine.

She couldn't bear this! It was far easier to face him than to be made so acutely conscious of him. She thought she could smell the faint masculine tang of him in the air—salty, musky, an intangible scent that denoted the man. Her thoughts lurched wildly to pheremomes—wasn't that what they called the faint olfactory signals given out by some male insects to attract females, and vice versa? Or was it pheremones? Pheronomes? Only a scientist would call scent an olfactory signal. Whatever, perhaps that was the source of Blaize's attraction. Unusually potent olfactory signals. Put like that, it was a far cry from the ravages of unrequited love.

He said silkily, 'I know you're awake.'

If he hadn't before he certainly did now. At the first sound of his voice she had jumped, giving herself away in that reflex action.

Forgetting to yawn, she sat up and scrambled away from him.

'Why were you pretending to be asleep?'

'I was hoping you'd leave me alone. I'm tired,' she said virtuously, refusing to meet his eyes as she tried to drag her tangled hair into some sort of order.

'You were as wound up as a spring.'

She gave him a scathing look and burrowed in her bag for a comb, found it and proceeded to use it ferociously on her hair.

'Don't do that,' he commanded, holding out his hand.

Stunned, she passed it over. He moved so that she sat between his outstretched legs with her back to him, and began to untangle the thick locks, using the comb with care and a smooth sweeping motion that should have been soothing.

She attacked, 'Did you want to be a hairdresser when you were young?'

He chuckled. 'No, but I've been wanting to touch this hair of yours ever since I saw it. It's springy, almost quivering with life, with strands like living silk.'

Unbearably stimulated by his nearness and his touch and the caressing note in his voice, she said stiffly, 'Like living barbed wire!'

'Rubbish. It's beautiful. So are you, for that matter.'

She snorted. 'Oh, yes, and pigs can fly!'

'Where did you get this thumping great inferiority complex?'

She turned and faced him down fiercely, her eyes snapping and vivid with anger. 'It's called being realistic,' she said curtly. 'I know I'm not beautiful because I've seen beautiful women all my life—I lived with one until I left home!—and I bear no resemblance to them. I have good skin, and that's it.'

'You have superb skin,' he told her lazily, his eyes examining as much of it as he could. 'More silk. As for beautiful, what's your idea of beauty?'

You, she thought achingly. You are the most beautiful thing I've ever seen, so magnificently confident in your masculinity, so kind to the children you took responsibility for, so physically splendid.

Aloud she said, 'Well, good skin, of course, and delicate bones, and a decent figure. Big eyes, long lashes. A sense of style, and graceful carriage.' Feminine hips. A bust that looks like a bust, not two insignificant mounds. And definitely not a height of just under six feet, and long, thin hands and feet.

'Is that what your mother looks like?'

She looked startled. Slowly, she said, 'Well, yes, I suppose so.'

'All right, let's go through them. We're agreed on the skin. Delicate bones—what is delicate? Fine, slender, fragile framework?'

It described her mother perfectly. 'Yes,' she said, even more slowly because she mistrusted the gleam in his eye. She stayed very still as he reached across to push the slightly sticky locks away from her face. His touch was doing strange things to her breathing.

'I admire delicate-looking women, but you know, I like a woman to match me as much as she is able. One has to be so careful with these fragile types. I like strength.' His hand slid caressingly along her cheek. 'Yes, it's there in the sweep of your jaw, your pointed, impertinent chin, the lovely high arc of your cheekbones— I wonder if a distant ancestor from Tartary gave you those? And your forehead, broad and serene, with your wild, wanton hair curling around it.'

As he spoke his fingers smoothed over the features he was enumerating. Entranced, Oriel sat without breathing, lashes drooping, her whole being concentrated on the touch of those gentle, knowledgeable fingers. His voice was deep, the crispness transformed into a smooth, sensual note, intimate, exciting.

'And your mouth,' he said, his thumb outlining the trembling contours. 'Do you know what that wide, soft mouth does to me every time I look at it, Oriel? I want to feel it on me, tasting me, warm and predatory and eager, doing the very things I want to do to you. I forget that I promised to leave you alone, I forget that until now my word has always been my bond. I wonder if you follow through on the assurances you don't even know you give. You look at me from under those heavy eyelids and my body clenches with need.'

Her heart almost stopped; she sat bathed in an aura of danger so pulsating with emotion that she thought she might faint.

He foiled her headlong flight by grabbing her wrist and hauling her down on to her knees, facing him. 'Good strong wrists,' he mused, capturing her other one and imprisoning them in a shackle of his lean hands. 'All that piano and tennis, no doubt. You'd make a good fencer. You have the grace and the style to carry it off.'

He was too close. Beneath lashes that were long and dark—and now she could see that they were not black, but darkest brown, with intriguing bronze tips—his eyes were startlingly grey with no hint of blue or green, a ring of darker grey about each dilated pupil. She yearned to touch the grain of his skin; the smooth, oiled silk of it was irresistibly tactile, and there was a fascinating roughness where his beard began. Her fingers itched to know whether it felt as interesting as it looked. His mouth, that conferer of intense pleasure, was beautifully sculptured, the upper lip a little narrower than the lower, both corners tucked in, a masterful combination of strength and beauty.

His jaw was clean and hard; more strength. Her fascinated gaze fell the length of his tanned throat to the Adam's apple, not inordinately prominent as some men's were. As her eyes surveyed it he swallowed.

Instantly her gaze flew back, to be snared by his. She flushed and tried to wrench free of his grip, saying in a constricted voice, 'Don't! I'm sorry.'

His hands tightened, holding her prisoner. 'Why? Because you looked? Or because you liked what you saw?'

Her tongue stole out to touch dry lips, then fled when she saw the flicker in his eyes as they followed the tiny movement. 'Blaize, don't,' she said, so softly that he had to bend his arrogant head to hear her.

'Don't what? Don't touch you?' His smile was without humour, a baring of the teeth that threatened more than it soothed. 'That's just it, Oriel. I want to touch you. And you want to touch me, don't you? I didn't force you to look at me, but you enjoyed it, just as I enjoy looking at you. It's about time you faced some facts. You've spent most of today flinching every time our eyes meet and looking away as though you'd just been introduced to Quasimodo.'

More colour licked across her skin. She thought feverishly that she could feel it rising from the pathetic mounds of her breasts right up to her hairline. Swallowing, she returned valiantly, 'Don't be an idiot. I find you very attractive, you must know that.'

'I do know it,' he said savagely. 'What I can't understand is why you so obviously are terrified by the whole thing. Although I think I'm beginning to. Any woman with a head full of inaccessible standards of physical beauty, standards it's physically impossible for her to reach, is bound to have trouble with her self-image. However, just in case you don't understand, I'll tell you again. And again, until at last you believe me. I find you profoundly, shatteringly attractive.'

Suddenly bitter, she said, 'It's easy to say, isn't it?'

His breath exhaled from between his teeth. Fascinated, she watched as his eyes darkened, narrowed. 'Are you so determined to cling to the protection of your inferiority complex?'

'Is that what it is? I suppose when you were the tallest in your class you were admired for it. I hated it. I was a freak.'

'All right, so it was painful to mature so much earlier than your classmates, although I can't help feeling that someone should have taken the time to convince you that height is something to enjoy. And I dare say that all through school the boys of your own age were too insecure to be interested in a woman so much taller than they were. But what have you been doing since then?'

He emphasised the question with a little jerk of her wrists. She stared at him, some part of her brain aware that, although he was holding her firmly, she was in no pain from his grip. He would hold a woman like that in love, she thought suddenly, so firmly yet with the utmost gentleness.

'Well?' he prompted. 'I can't believe that every man you've ever met is so insecure that he needs the reassurance of a woman shorter than himself. Or that so many have taken you at your mother's valuation——' He stopped, and she saw him make the connection. 'Yes, of course,' he said slowly, his eyes keen and hard as they surveyed her stiff face. 'Because your mother's valuation is also yours, isn't it?'

She shrugged. 'It's also everyone else's valuation. Look, I don't want you to think I'm some drag who has to sit at home every night. I go out, I enjoy men's company, I——'

'How many men have you become serious about?'

Stiffly she said, 'That's my business.'

His sharp gaze was pinning her mercilessly, flaying through the defences that pain had built around her heart. 'What do you do to them when they start to fall in love with you, Oriel? Freeze them off, as you're trying to freeze me off? It won't work. I know that beneath that serene innocence there's a woman of powerful emotions and passions. Emotions and passions I want.'

'You said there wouldn't be any repetitions,' she said breathlessly. 'You promised.'

'I lied.'

Like one enchanted, she watched his head come towards her, his features sculpted out of bronze, the delectable lower lip held slightly away from that thinner top one. Before his face swam in her vision she thought fancifully that his top lip denoted his will—implacable, unsparing—the bottom the sensual side of his nature.

And then their mouths touched, and she was no longer capable of thought. Weighted by an intolerable desire, they sank down on to the rug. The sun warmed her shoulders, heated her hair, and the dazzlement of the day combined with his enslavement of her senses to hold her prisoner. Almost fainting with pleasure, the only movement she could discern was the leaping of her pulses through her warm, lax body. Apart from their mouths they touched nowhere else but their hands.

'So sweet,' he whispered on a shaken sigh. 'Release me from my promise, Oriel.'

A faint remnant of common sense made her lips form the word no.

'Then I'll have to kiss you until you give me what I want,' he threatened.

'The children . . .'

'Playing pirates. They'll be happy until we call them. Tell me that I can kiss you again.'

She gave a half sob. 'Why? You don't keep your promises. Why do you want my permission to do something you're going to do anyway?'

His laugh was a warm breath on her lips. 'Because I want it. I need to hear you say it.'

'Surrender?'

'Perhaps. But in this war there are no losers.'

It took all her will-power, but she forced her laden lashes up, saw the glazed silver of his gaze lit from within by a sensuality so intense that she was burning up in it. She said thickly, 'I won't. You might not lose, but I will.'

'Why?'

But she was aware of how close she had come to giving herself away. She shook her head and scrambled to her feet, and he let her go, saying casually, as though they had never exchanged that kiss, 'One day, Oriel, not too far distant, you'll give me what I want.'

'This is sexual harassment!'

He laughed at her. 'Have I said I'll fire you if you don't give in to my wicked desires?'

'No, but you can make my life impossible.'

He got to his feet in a single lithe movement, towering over her in a warning that was only implied, but very obvious. 'You could stop me,' he pointed out in a steely tone, 'by simply saying no and meaning it.'

She bit her lip but parried, 'I can want you and not want you to kiss me. For you it's an amusement, something to pass your holiday away pleasantly. But for me—have you thought how it might affect me?'

'You have no idea how anything affects you,' he said cruelly. 'You are about as naïve as the normal thirteen-year-old girl. Is that it—are you a coward, Oriel? Do you really want me to leave you alone?'

'Yes!' she cried passionately, wounded and angry.

He looked at her, his handsome face hard and unyielding. 'Sure, Oriel?' His voice was silky-soft, almost soundless.

A gull called a warning. Sand granules on her legs began to itch slightly. A vagrant breeze lifted the heavy, silver-backed leaves of the trees above her and moved them slightly, then released them back into sleep. Simon gave a bloodthirsty yell, collapsing into laughter when Sarah responded with a ferocious war chant. Oriel was very still, her face pale and tight and bitter.

'Is this what you want?' Blaize pressed. 'If you tell me now to stop pestering you I will, permanently.'

It will be for the best, her mind told her quivering heart.

'Oriel?'

Harshly, the words impeded, she said, 'I want you to leave me alone.'

She didn't expect him to turn and walk away, as though he couldn't bear to look at her, but that was what he did. Numbly, she watched the lean figure in faded shorts and T-shirt stride without a backward glance across the hot sand and disappear around the rocks at the end of the beach.

Still staring after him, she heard the children's yells of greeting, and a rousing chorus of 'Sixteen men on a dead man's chest', with the shattering feeling that she had indeed shown herself to be a coward, let something very rare and beautiful slip through her fingers. No, had wilfully smashed it, fouling it with her own stupidity.

Then she thought bracingly, You see, he did only want to amuse himself. Otherwise he'd have tried to talk you out of it. You've had a narrow escape. And in time this stupid, totally unwanted love will die and you'll be able to look at him with nothing more than liking and respect.

But, You're a fool, her heart jeered. A fool, a cowardly fool. You've always been afraid, too frightened to let anyone close in case they found you wanting. He saw. He knows. 'Freeze them off.' Just as you froze him off.

Face set, she began to pack the remnants of their picnic away.

CHAPTER SEVEN

BACK at the house Oriel took Sarah up to her bedroom and helped her wash her hair in the shower. Sarah prattled about her wonderful day, submitted to a vigorous towel-drying of her hair and asked if she could wear her prettiest dress to greet the guests. She would eat an early dinner on a tray but was allowed to stay up until eight.

Oriel picked up a comb and kissed the little button nose. 'Yes, of course you can.'

'Can I stay up until nine o'clock?' she pleaded.

'No.'

'Why not? Simon's going to. He doesn't have to go to bed till eleven o'clock, he told me.'

'You know what Uncle Blaize said, cherub, so don't twist that pretty face up into a scowl.' Oriel began to comb the fine tresses into order, firmly repressing memories of the afternoon and how it had felt to have Blaize tend her hair.

Sarah sighed, but she was a biddable child who responded well to firmness. She said tentatively, 'Can I see what you're going to wear?'

'Yes, of course.' In spite of her convictions Oriel knew she was going to wear the Decadence outfit, and without a bra. Just once in her life she wanted to look daring, even slightly wicked. Aloud, she said, 'Bring a book along and you can read while I shower and do my hair.'

For, much to her delight, Sarah was now able to read some of the simpler books in her shelves.

On the way to Oriel's bedroom Sarah asked even more tentatively, 'Can I sit on your bed and watch you get dressed? Sometimes Mummy let me do that, and she used to put a tiny bit of eyeshadow and some perfume on me, and Daddy would say, "And who's this beautiful woman? I think I'll take her out tonight instead of you, Sue." And Mummy would pretend to cry, and I would tell him he was a bad man to make her cry and he had to take Mummy out.'

Her voice wobbled ominously. Oriel leaped down and tucked her hand in hers, afraid to speak in case she said the wrong thing.

Sarah clung. After a moment she whispered, 'Oriel, where are they now? Mummy and Daddy? Is it dark? Are they together? They wouldn't like to be all by themselves, Oriel.'

Oriel sat down on the stair and pulled her into her lap. 'Dear heart,' she said, stroking the damp hair off the tragic, bewildered little face, 'I'm sure they're together, and I'm certain it isn't dark.'

'Why did God take them away? He doesn't need them as much as we do. Simon misses them too. And so does Uncle Blaize. When we came home from the fun'ral I sat on his knee and I was crying and Simon started to cry too, and Uncle Blaize cuddled Simon too—and Oriel, Uncle Blaize cried too, I saw the tears in his eyes. I didn't know grown-ups could cry, Oriel. Oriel, why did God take them away from us?'

'Oh, darling, we don't know why He does some of the things He does. We just have to believe that He knows best. I know it's hard to understand, even grown-ups don't understand, but darling, the hurting will go away some day, I promise, and you'll be able to remember them without feeling so sad.'

Sarah pressed her hot little face into Oriel's breast, weeping, seeking comfort. Her heart aching at the tragedy of it, Oriel's too-vivid imagination supplied the scene when the three of them had mourned their loss. She leaned her cheek against the soft, baby-fine hair and rocked back and forth, uncaring of the footsteps in the hall below. They slowed, but she didn't look up, and immediately they faded away towards the back of the house.

After a while Sarah's sobs died away and she sat up, saying drowsily, 'I was nearly asleep.' Her arms wound around Oriel's neck as she gave her a swift kiss on the cheek. 'You're nice,' she said. 'I like you better than my last governess. She was grumpy and she didn't pat my back when I cried and she was always very happy.'

Familiar with the brisk, impersonal cheerfulness that was the trademark of nurses and teachers, Oriel understood exactly what Sarah meant. Returning her hug, she replied, 'I like you too. Now, how about coming up to my room so I can get ready for this party?'

Still sniffing but apparently comforted, Sarah agreed, her hand tucked firmly into Oriel's as they turned off the landing.

She watched eagerly as Oriel made her preparations, and when finally she was ready said, 'Oh, you look so pretty!' her voice awestruck as she watched Oriel parade about the room in an imitation of a model's smooth glide. 'Like those dolls in the shop windows.'

Oriel grinned as she made an elaborate curtsy. She allowed herself one look over her shoulder at the raspberry and white skirt and the thin white top. Surveying the bare, sleek lines of shoulder and breast and waist, she wondered for a horrible panicky moment whether she was being ridiculous, whether she was too thin to wear the clinging garment with any panache. Morbidly her eyes searched for rib-bones, until she realised what she was doing and frowned with vexation, looking hastily away.

'Thank you,' she said gravely.

A week ago Kathy had come home from Russell with a lipstick the exact colour of the skirt. As Oriel applied it she heard Blaize's voice in her mind. Like kissing a flower, he had said... Pain struck a hammer blow to her heart. She saw her eyes dilate, then narrow, the blue draining into darkness. What had she done when she'd rejected him?

A knock on the door straightened her back. Her first breath was like a dagger in her heart, but she forced her mouth into some semblance of a smile and called, 'Come in.'

It was Simon, very elegant in the outfit all trendy teens were wearing that summer—dark trousers and a round-necked, vaguely Cossack shirt with long, full sleeves caught into a band at each wrist. The fine white cotton set off his tan to full advantage and emphasised the colour of his hair and eyes with superb effect.

'You look stunning,' Oriel said sincerely.

He grinned. 'So do you. Very smart.'

'What about me?'

He walked around Sarah, now standing beside the bed, and pretended to survey her. 'Choice, Sarah. Get another couple of teeth and you'll be the belle of the ball.'

She pulled a hideous face at him, then gave a hop and ran across the room. 'Come on,' she urged. 'I want to see the party.'

'After you've had your dinner.' Oriel smiled at Simon and said innocently, 'I wonder if Kathy has anything extra on Sarah's tray. Hop down and bring it up here, will you, Sim, and we'll have a six o'clock feast.'

Kathy had considered the never-ending hunger of adolescent boys, for there were two plates on the tray, and far more food than Sarah would be able to eat.

'You and Kathy are two in a million,' Simon said, astounding Oriel by giving her a quick kiss on the cheek before settling down to demolish his share.

Half an hour later they took the empty trays back to the kitchen, washed the dishes, then set off on a tour around the house. Kathy had retired to her flat to dress, and Blaize, so Simon informed her, was once more holed up in the library with James Weatherall.

So they were free to wander through the rooms and admire the great bowls of hibiscus flowers that lit up selected corners with their saturated reds and iridescent golds, crimson and pink and maroon, amber and ochre and saffron, silken petals burning with the fierce heat of their tropical homelands.

The house flowed together to provide an ambience for every taste, from the wide terraces with their views of the sea and the swimming-pool to the cosy comfort of the small sitting-room with its sofas and chairs, ideal for those who wanted a restful party. The design was brilliant, for as well as being a comfortable holiday home it was perfect for entertaining.

For both Simon and Sarah the *pièce de résistance* was the food set out on the screened terrace, a long buffet of every delicious resource the region offered.

'There's going to be crayfish and fish and all sorts of shellfish,' Simon offered, in the tones of one who could hardly wait. 'They're in the chiller-room. But it looks just like a banquet, doesn't it?'

It did indeed. Kathy had arranged the food with a casual country sophistication that made a glowing, beautiful picture suiting both the occasion and the setting.

From the doorway Blaize said, 'So this is where you all are. I should have known it would be with the food! Let's have a look at you.'

Sarah ran across and pirouetted in front of him, saying eagerly, 'Oriel did my hair a new way, with her drier. Do you like it?'

'It looks charming,' he said, touching the bell of hair around her chubby little face. His gaze bypassed Oriel altogether and came to rest on Simon. Those devastating brows rose. 'Exotic, Sim.'

He grinned. 'Just because you're stuck in a groove it doesn't mean I have to be too. After all, anyone can wear a silk Italian shirt, but it would take a brave man to wear this outfit and get away with it.'

'You look very good.' Blaize's eyes measured the straight young figure. 'I think you're going to be as tall as your father by the time you've finished growing. You can certainly wear clothes as well as he did.'

He couldn't have said anything that gratified Simon more. Flushing, he said awkwardly, 'Thank you.'

'Let's go and have something to drink while we wait for our guests.'

But Sarah stopped him from turning completely away by saying urgently, 'What about Oriel? Don't you like her dress?'

'Of course,' he said with cool and completely snubbing courtesy. 'Oriel always looks charming.'

Satisfied, Sarah took his hand and went with him, but Simon, older and more observant, sent Oriel a puzzled glance. Like her, he had seen that his uncle hadn't looked at her once. A cold pang in her heart made her catch her breath, but she managed to produce a teasing smile, and saw Simon relax.

He bowed and held out his arm. 'Madam,' he said with a flourish, 'allow me to escort you.'

Smiling, she laid her hand on the white material of his shirt and they followed the other two out on to the terrace.

It was the beginning of an evening of agony for Oriel, a time when she realised just what she had done by rejecting so wholeheartedly whatever it was that Blaize had offered. Not that he was rude; he didn't need to be. He introduced her with that same chilling, aloof courtesy to all his guests—local farmers and fishermen and their wives and girlfriends, many of the other holidaymakers with permanent baches around the Bay of Islands, friends up from Auckland—'to provide the locals with some amusement', as James Weatherall told her, *sotto voce*—in all ways he couldn't have been more polite, more interested in making sure she had a wonderful party—or more distant.

The distance she could have borne; what tore her feelings to shreds was the way members of her sex watched him, the eager anticipation in the eyes of the unattached women and more than a few of the attached ones, and the open avidity with which they responded to his presence, the undignified manoeuvring to get near him. And when they had caught his attention, the coquettish laughter and inviting body language with which they tried to keep it.

He was a consummate flirt, the raw edges of power muted just enough to smooth down the danger, his overwhelming sexuality not tamed at all by the superb silk shirt and narrow trousers. It made Oriel sick and furious to see the way women preened when he gave them that devastating smile; she felt like clawing it from his face.

The violence and wildness of her emotions frightened her. After a short while she refused to look at him. Even that didn't work. Somehow, she knew all the time exactly where he was. And whenever, heartsick and frustrated, her eyes glittering with suppressed feelings, she managed to make her way into another room he seemed to find his way there too, although she knew he couldn't be following her.

She should have been enjoying herself. Almost without exception everyone was welcoming and pleasant, eager to make the most of the occasion, and the evening had that fizzing, sparkling atmosphere that assured its success. Thanks to Kathy's discerning eye, Oriel was dressed with exactly the right casual chic, and she had no difficulty in talking to whoever she met while she kept an eye on Sarah, who had quite a few friends among the partygoers. Oriel's height helped there, as apart from a few of the men she was the tallest person in the room.

Although as the evening wore on her eyes fell on another very tall woman—blonde and built on magnificent lines, she had unusually pale eyes that gave her a striking, compelling air, set as they were in dark lashes and brows. Probably dyed, Oriel thought snidely, envying the woman her deep bosom and splendid curves.

By dint of the utmost concentration she managed to give a fair imitation of someone who was enjoying herself. It was not the sort of evening for deep conversation, and at this superficial level she could hold her own. She followed Sarah slowly through the house, arriving eventually at the sitting-room, and there she drank sparingly of an excellent New Zealand champagne while a tall dark young man with the face of a handsome bandit and laughing, speculative green eyes flirted casually with her.

Until she saw Sarah cover a gap-toothed yawn. Then she said politely, 'I'm sorry, Mr...'

'André,' he said sadly. 'André Hunter. Have I made such a little impression on you, beautiful Miss Radford, that you can't even remember my name? I'm shattered.'

Horrified, she looked up, but surprised a lurking gleam in his smile that made her laugh. 'I'm lousy with names,' she said, 'but I should have remembered yours, shouldn't I? Mr Hunter——'

'André, please.'

'André, then, I have to take young Sarah to bed before she falls asleep on the floor.'

'I'll wait for you,' he said cheerfully.

She hesitated, then gave an infinitesimal shrug. A month ago she would have been shy, almost afraid of him; it was amazing what falling in love could do. She didn't care what anyone else but Blaize thought of her, and in a strange way it set her free.

So she gave the man beside her a sweet, empty smile, set down her glass and made her way across the room, to find that her charge was talking to the Valkyrie with the ease of old friends.

'Here's Oriel now,' she said, her small face splitting into a grin.

The blonde woman was warm and welcoming. 'We haven't been introduced,' she said, 'although I feel I know a lot about you! I'm Lora Duncan, and you are Oriel Radford, who's going to be Sarah's friend.'

Her sensitivity in not referring to her as Sarah's new mother, as several other women had, made Oriel forget her inadequacy in the matter of curves. She returned the smile and the greeting, and asked politely, 'Are you a local, or have you come up from Auckland?'

'Oh, we're locals. My husband and I live on the other side of Paihia.'

'They've got a nenormous station with cows with big, floppy ears, and two sorts of goats and deers,' Sarah informed her in tones throbbing with envy. 'And some sheep. They make yoghurt and cheese to sell in Australia and they live in a lovely old house with red tiles on the roof. And they've got a little baby boy. He's called Matthew Alexander Duncan, but they call him Matthew. He smiled at me last Christmas.'

'He's not a baby any more, sweetheart,' Lora Duncan said a little ruefully. 'He runs around and talks all the time and is certain he can ride. Matt put him up on a pony before he could even walk, and now he wants to go out with him on the station all the time.'

Oriel suppressed a pang of envy, as Sarah said importantly, 'That's Uncle Matt over there talking to Uncle Blaize, see? No, not there, Oriel, over by the windows.'

Reluctantly Oriel followed the chubby pointing finger. Matt Duncan was as tall as Blaize but leaner in build, with hair the most intriguing mixture of golds and ambers and rusts blended to form a fascinating marmalade effect. Together, he and Blaize took the breath away. They looked like great tawny cats, superbly at ease, magnificently confident in their untrammelled masculinity.

Oriel took a deep breath and said steadily, 'I see him.'

'Wonderful, aren't they?' Lora Duncan's voice was soft and wry. 'Apart each is fantastic, but together—they make your mouth water!'

Oriel watched as Matt Duncan's eyes caught his wife's, and they exchanged smiles, slow and significant. Clearly the Duncans had a very satisfying marriage. Then her gaze was captured too, pinned by the silver rapier of Blaize's. She tried to drag her eyes away, but he held them effortlessly, his own cold and merciless. Matt Duncan said something to him, and they began to move through the crowd towards them.

'Of course,' Lora said in her warm voice, 'we must look pretty stunning too. A Valkyrie and a—well, you're something else again. Melusine, perhaps, with those fascinating eyes? Where did they come from?'

'My father,' Oriel said, glad of the opportunity to look back at the other woman. 'Thank you.'

Lora grinned. 'And I'd kill for a figure like that, so slender and sinuous and graceful. Mine, alas, is altogether too lush—all bosom and hips.'

Oriel's mouth fell open. 'I was envying you,' she said. 'I'm as straight as a lath.'

They both burst into laughter, and Lora said wryly, shaking her magnificent blonde head, 'What do they do to us women, that we spend all our time wanting what we haven't got? I'm going to stop it here and now.'

The men arrived and Oriel was introduced to Matt Duncan. She liked him, although she found his golden regard uncomfortably penetrating, and she didn't altogether relish the way he watched her. He was lovely to Sarah, though, swinging her up in his arms to give her a big kiss. She kissed him back enthusiastically, but spoiled the effect with another yawn.

'Bedtime,' Blaize said. 'Have you had dinner?'

'Yes, Oriel and Sim and me had it on a tray in Oriel's bedroom. I had a chicken leg and avocado and prawns and then I had a meringue and a drink of lemonade.' Sarah yawned again and held out her arms to Blaize. 'Will you come and kiss me goodnight?'

'Yes, in a few minutes.'

He put her down and sent an unsmiling glance to Oriel. 'Thank you,' he said formally.

Relegated to her place, she waited while Sarah kissed Lora, then set off with her through the crowds of people who were all clearly having a fascinating and highly enjoyable time, and up the stairs to Sarah's room with its bed like a racing car and the beloved books lying about.

Ten minutes later, clad in cotton shortie pyjamas, Sarah hurtled into her bed. She chose Maurice Sendak's *Where The Wild Things Are*, so Oriel read the story of the boy who sailed his boat over the sea to become king of the wild things, then returned to the security of his own home and his parents.

'I like that,' Sarah said sleepily. 'I like you, Oriel. Goodnight.'

She held up her arms. Oriel kissed her and held her for a moment, her aching heart enjoying the comfort of the warm, sturdy little body.

'Goodnight, sweetheart,' she said softly. 'Sleep tight. You can come into my room in the morning if you like when you wake up, because everyone else will probably be tired and a bit grumpy if you wake them too early.'

'Not Uncle Blaize,' Sarah said with such total conviction that Oriel was convinced.

A final kiss and Oriel settled her back on the pillow. She stood for a moment smiling down at the almost sleeping child, then leaned down to switch on the small night-light. As she turned to go out she saw Blaize standing in the doorway. Something in the curious stillness of his stance warned her that he had been there for a while. Her heart leapt, but she managed to hide the welter of emotions by assuming a calm, mildly interested expression as she came towards him.

'Wait for me,' he ordered.

She obeyed, watching him as he went across and kissed his niece's forehead. The long lashes fluttered, Sarah said his name in a drowsy little voice, and then she turned over on to her side, clearly lost in the fathomless sleep of childhood.

He straightened, his tall frame intimidating in the darkened room. Oriel stood motionless as he closed the door. At the bottom of the stairs he said coldly, 'Can you check on Simon, make sure he gets off at eleven? He's too old to be kissed goodnight, but he likes someone to come in and see he's all right. His mother always used to.'

His manner, his voice, chilled her to the bone. Quietly she nodded. 'I want to talk to you about what you've told Sarah about her parents' death, but I can do that later.'

'Tell me now.'

Oriel revealed the unhappy little scene on the stairs, ending, 'I don't want to contradict anything you've said about what has happened to them, but she obviously finds the thought of them being alone or in the dark distressing.'

'I went past while you were comforting her. You seemed to have it well in hand, so I left you to it. She's afraid of the dark, of course.'

His voice was tired. She remembered Sarah's artless confidence about the tears in his eyes after the funeral.

'Just ease her fears as much as possible,' he said, and in the same voice continued, 'Oh, and be careful with André Hunter. He's generally considered to be rather dangerous when it comes to women.'

'André Hunter?' The sudden change of subject threw her entirely. Her sluggish brain was disorientated by his nearness, her heart was clamouring for her to give in, to tell him that there was nothing she wanted more than to be welcomed back into the warmth of his favour.

'Come now, Oriel, don't pretend.' His eyes were crystalline, as cold as the icebergs in the southern seas. 'You were enjoying his company very much. He's attractive, and he's rich and he's going to be much richer, but he has a bad reputation with women. However, just in case you think you might get more from him, the contract you signed doesn't make any exceptions, not even for marriage.'

His scathing voice drove the colour painfully from her skin. After a moment she gathered enough poise to say, 'For heaven's sake, I was just talking to the man! Who the hell do you think you are——?'

'I'm your employer,' he said brutally, 'with a vested interest in your efficiency. I don't want a nanny who's useless because she's pregnant, or broken-hearted over a rake like André Hunter.'

The casual, pointedly cruel insults heated her blood to boiling-point. Through teeth clenched so tightly she thought they might snap she hissed, 'You have a bloody nerve. You may have bought my services, but you haven't bought me! I'll talk to whoever I want to, and there's nothing you can do about it.'

'Oh, you can talk to him,' he said with indifference. 'Tease him as much as you like—you're a consummate tease, aren't you, with those wicked eyes and that wide, innocent mouth? Just don't sleep with him, or break your heart over him. As for buying you—that, my dear, is exactly what I've done. Your services, your time, your efforts. You are mine. And if you don't want to cause André Hunter a considerable amount of trouble, leave him alone.'

Sickened by his stony viciousness, she turned away.

'Where are you going?' His voice cracked like a whip.

'Up to my room.'

She didn't hear him move, but she hadn't taken two steps when her arm was taken in a grip just short of painful. 'I said I owned you,' he said in her ear, his voice lethal. 'And I want you where I can see you, Oriel. So you're not going up to your room to sulk, you're coming with me.'

Fuming, she sent him a look of pure hatred, her eyes narrowed into slits of molten blue, her lips pressed so tightly together that they were white.

'If you come back like that, people will think I've kissed all your lipstick off,' he said, coldly amused. 'You'd better go up and replace it.'

Ignoring her furious protests, he escorted her up to her door, waiting outside while she carefully filled in the colour with a trembling hand. She took as long as she dared, pressing her hands to the bench in front of the bathroom mirror, wondering with alarm who the woman in the mirror was with her raging blue eyes and the sullen, full mouth glossed with scarlet. She looked totally different, bold, angry and more alive than she had ever seen herself.

Only Blaize had the power to do this to her, strike sparks off her so that she was incandescent with emotion, flaming with an energy she had never tapped before.

From outside the room he called her name, impatience clipping the syllables, and she gave a last fulminating stare at her reflection and went out to meet him, her head held so high that she felt an ache in her neck and shoulders.

Something leapt into full-blown life in the shadowed eyes that watched her come through the doorway, something that raged unchecked for a second until his massive will-power called it under control and vanquished it. She walked past him without touching him, looking at him, yet she could feel his attention like a gas flare about her, searing her nerves, setting every cell in her body aflame with triumph.

Hating him for his arrogance, his cruelty, she was savagely glad that he wanted her, glad that her presence affected him in ways she was only now beginning to understand.

People watched them as they came back into the room, some openly, some with interested sideways glances. Oriel met glittering, wicked green eyes, and smiled, but she quashed her first savagely defiant instinct to go across to where André Hunter lounged against a wall and lifted his champagne glass to her, watching her with that sly amusement.

Besides, her saner, more sensible self was struggling to be heard through the pain and the anger. It would be utterly stupid to antagonise Blaize any more than she had done. She had signed that contract, and for better or worse he was going to hold her to it, so it was much more sensible to make it for better, not worse.

Even more important than the contract was the promise she had made to Sarah.

Normally she hated confrontations and fights; the fact that this one stimulated her, made her feel infinitely more alive than she had ever been before, was probably the result of her inexperience. But it wouldn't be good for Sarah to live in a situation where there were constant battles.

Unfortunately, while her common sense made soothing noises and came up with platitudes and calm reason, her anger, bone-deep, unresolved, bubbled away, feeding her adrenalin rush, giving her eyes a sultry, smoky intensity, touching her skin with fugitive colour, lifting her chin.

She felt it in him too. For the rest of that nightmarish party, even as he refused to let her leave his side, she sensed his feral desire to be free of them all so that he could give rein to his emotions. She should have been terrified, but it was not terror that stiffened her spine and touched her cheeks with colour.

Although he smiled frequently, his anger gave him an air of brooding intensity that was blazingly magnetic to the many women who sent Oriel sharp, envious little glances. Kept at his side like a potentate's favourite handmaiden, she was bound together with him in an orb of sizzling energy, separated from everyone else by a force-field.

Ten minutes after Simon went up to bed she slid away, and this time Blaize let her go. By now her foot was aching slightly, so she limped up the stairs and knocked on Simon's door; a sleepy voice bade her come in, but she was met with a broad if exhausted smile when she asked, 'Everything all right?'

'Fine. Great party, isn't it?'

'Fantastic,' she retorted drily. 'Goodnight.'

''Night,' he said, only barely covering a yawn. 'See you in the morning.'

'Not too early, I hope.'

He laughed. 'Not a chance. I'm not getting up until midday.'

'Good thinking, Ninety-nine.'

He laughed, and she shut the door and went down the stairs. A couple were just settling themselves in a secluded nook in the passage; she went past awkwardly, thinking with some distaste that at least her mother had made sure that she would never think of making love on the stairs during a party. With the woman's giggle in her ears she paced on down, girding her loins for another period of purgatory.

She fully expected to find Blaize lying in wait, but he was nowhere in sight. Quickly, before he had a chance to catch up with her, she walked down the hall to the back door, slipping past the lasiandra hedge, the purple, silken flowers glowing more vividly than any royal robes, and on down the darkened pathway to the pool.

White tobacco flowers scented the air, mingling with the evocative fragrance of the port-wine magnolia and the heavy, musky scent of the Queen of the Night blooms, tiny and inconspicuous yet almost over-powering, floating over the gardens in sensuous evocation of the tropics.

There had been swimming earlier on, but now the pool was empty of people. Water was lapping gently against the dark sides, water that Kathy had sprinkled with gardenia blossoms, hundreds of them, lying in swathes of white on the surface, their heavy scent erotic and clinging in the warm, salty air.

Oriel stood for a long time, breathing deeply, her eyes fixed unseeingly on the water, but at last she shivered, turning to go back. A dark shadow detached itself from the wall beneath the climbing rose. Her hand clenched at her breast, then relaxed. This man was just as tall but not as massively built as Blaize.

'A little over the top, but highly effective, isn't it? Who'd have thought of Blaize revelling in romantic conceits?' It was André Hunter, his voice amused and more than a little curious.

'I think the idea was his housekeeper's,' Oriel told him levelly. Made uneasy by Blaize's threats, she said stiffly, 'I'd better go back inside.'

'Can I help?' She looked at him in surprise and he gestured at her foot. 'I notice you're limping slightly, and the path, though very pretty, is a little uneven.'

'No, I'm all right, it's almost better now.'

They paced back through the scented darkness, and just before they reached the lights and the music and the tension, André said, 'Tell me, are you Blaize's lady?'

'No.'

'I see. Then I can give in to my masculine instincts and kiss the most intriguing woman I've met in a long time.'

She took a hasty step backwards, and came down heavily on her foot. An epithet was wrenched from her; she flailed around, clutching wildly at him.

He grabbed her and supported her against the lean elegance of his body, demanding, 'Are you all right?'

'It's fine—you just surprised me, that's all.' Testing the foot, she wriggled it, saying in a relieved voice as she drew away, 'No harm done.'

But the incident had given her an idea. She would not go back into that house and be forced to stay beside Blaize. Now that both children were in bed she had fulfilled her duties, and she had a perfectly good excuse for going up to her room.

'You know,' he said, regarding her thoughtfully, 'I don't usually meet with that reaction when I suggest kissing someone. I must be losing my touch.'

A choke of laughter escaped her. 'Sorry, I was just surprised.'

'Why? I imagine every time you go out into a garden at night some man wants to kiss you. You have an eminently kissable mouth.'

He spoke with an air of calm reason that made her retort tartly, 'If there happens to be a step-ladder about, some men no doubt would.'

'I think you're just the right height. Would you like me to demonstrate?'

'No,' she parried, very firmly, although he won a reluctant smile. If this was what a rake was like, she hoped she'd meet some more during her life. She wouldn't want to fall in love with André Hunter or anyone like him; he was fun and charming, but like Blaize he was wrapped in that aura of danger, a man whose will it wouldn't pay to cross. However, she knew she was in no peril from him. He was flirting and he was doing it very well, and she was grateful for his easy sang-froid.

'Pity. Still, if you're adamant,' his voice altered, became brisk and authoritative, 'we'd better get something done to that foot.'

'No, it's fine, I haven't damaged it further, but I think I'll go up to my room now. The wretched thing swells when it's had enough.'

Music surged from the house. 'And if they're going to dance,' he said with complete understanding, 'it's not going to be much fun for you.'

She had the uncomfortable feeling that those wicked green eyes were far too perceptive, but she smiled and said, 'Exactly. I'll go in through the back way.'

She intended him to leave her, but he said promptly, 'I'll come with you.'

In spite of all her urgings and protestations he wouldn't leave her; furthermore, he insisted on hooking his arm around her waist and taking as much of her weight as was possible. She could have got there quite easily herself, but here, she thought with a hint of irritation, was another protective male. Perhaps the area attracted them!

At least she was almost sure they got to her room without anyone seeing them. Exasperation, however, came perilously close to annoyance when she realised that he wasn't going to leave her and go back to the party. No, he insisted she lie down on her bed while unhurriedly he got her face-cloth and wetted it under the cold tap and brought it back into the bedroom to tuck around her foot.

'To stop the swelling,' he said, eyeing the length of her leg with unhidden appreciation.

Half angrily, she said, 'Look, you've been very kind, but I don't need you any more now.'

'I'm desolated,' he said with a curious half-smile. 'Why are you so nervous? I promise you I don't go in for rape.'

His frankness startled her. She flushed but said quickly, 'I didn't for a moment think you did.'

'But you don't want me here. Why? Because you were lying before, and you are Blaize's woman? And because Blaize is not noted for his eagerness to share, especially his——'

Through gritted teeth she interrupted, 'I am not——'

'I don't think I believe you. However, I'll go.' André looked at her with amusement and something like regret. 'Sleep well, Oriel. I'd ask you to dream of me, but I'm sure there'll be another man in your mind during the night.'

CHAPTER EIGHT

ORIEL felt like speeding André on his way with a well-placed shoe, but he finally left the room, and she collapsed back on to the pillow with a horrified sigh. A quick glance at her watch showed that he had been in the room for almost twenty minutes; shivering, she recalled Blaize's face as he had warned her off André.

By the time she got into her nightgown she was exhausted. Turning the light out, she locked the door and lay back on the sheets, willing the sounds of the party to dull and die, and blessed sleep to claim her.

She was still awake when the last car lights dwindled and died away behind the hills, when the last note of the last outboard engine faded into the heavy air behind the headland. It was another unbearably sticky night; long ago she had pushed off the bedclothes but found no relief. Now she walked across to the window, leaning out in an effort to get some coolness.

It was very still, otherwise she probably wouldn't have heard Kathy's voice, pitched perhaps a little louder than normal. Of course, she and Ned would be walking back to their flat, and the heavy atmosphere trapped their voices, making them reverberate.

'Well, thank heavens it all went off so well,' Kathy said. The yawn that followed was obvious.

Oriel smiled and began to draw her head back in.

Her husband made some comment, his voice too indistinct for the words to register.

'Oh, he always thanks me.' Kathy's normally pleasant tones were acid. 'He even kept Madam McLean waiting

148

while he did it; she wanted to be off quickly, before he changed his mind, I think.'

Another muted reply, but Kathy's sniff was obvious. Oriel knew she should walk away, but a miserable need to know more kept her riveted to the window.

'Of course it was a set-up. She's been after him for years, and her sister deliberately left her here. Well, even if she gets what she wants, I hope she hasn't any ideas about it being permanent. Blaize can marry any woman in the world, why would he want a nasty-tempered baggage like her, even if she does look like the Queen of Sheba? He's too fastidious. No, she's a flash in the pan, that one.'

Oriel remembered the McLean woman, a stunning redhead in her early thirties, with a body that should have been voluptuous but was fashionably svelte, kept that way no doubt by rigid dieting. She had been one of the coterie of women who had sent Blaize those flickering, darting little looks of appreciation.

Oriel's nails bit into her palms. Carefully she unclenched her fingers. It was nothing to do with her. She had turned him down unequivocally. He could do whatever he wanted, and if that entailed sleeping with a woman who was as obvious as 'Madam McLean', then the decision was his.

She fought and barely controlled the black tide of rage and fury. With a blazing certainty that owed nothing to logic, she realised at last that just as she was his, he was hers. In a moment that was terrifying in its irrevocable nature she claimed him as her man, body, mind and soul, hers for eternity. She would kill him if he spent the rest of the night in anyone else's bed.

On a shattered sob she turned and fled down the stairs, oddly surprised to feel no pain in her foot. Impelled by a feverish need for action, she walked out through the unlocked back door, down the path by the night-scented flowers, their fragrances mingling to mock her tormented thoughts with their sensuous evocation of love and passion.

The water in the pool beckoned her heated body; she stood a long time staring into it, wondering if it was an optical illusion that made it seem as though the water gave off a haze of steam. Sweat clung to her body, making her feel unclean.

Without giving herself time to think she tore off her nightgown and lowered herself into the pool, expecting to shiver with coolness, only to find that the water that lapped around her sleek, tanned thighs was as warm as the blood that pounded through her body. The scent of the gardenias rose through her brain, the fumes dazing, almost overpowering. She slid silently in, pushing aside the glowing flowers with her arms, stroking smoothly, her whole being centred on the sensuous swirl of the water across her fevered skin, her body crying for a lover.

Just when she realised that she wasn't alone she never knew. The knowledge wasn't instant, a sudden blow to her solitude. It crept slowly into her consciousness, teasing, tormenting, tantalising, a subtle instinct that should have frightened her.

But it was as though she was caught in a spell, an enchantment of the brain and the senses, captive to a master's will. Swimming without sound through the water, she saw the drops as they flicked from her arms like crystals in the pagan, primordial light of the moon, and knew that the man she loved was watching her, desiring her with an intensity that matched her own.

She didn't look to where he waited in the darkness beneath the white flowers of the stephanotis twining through the pergola. Not by any sign did she show that she knew of his presence. Later, when the madness was over, she was convinced that she didn't even think during that timeless, mindless period. She existed; she felt; she wanted. Nothing else penetrated the cocoon of her needs and the dangerous magic of the night, not caution, nor common sense, nor the instinct of self-preservation. For that time out of time she was woman, and he was man, nothing else mattered.

She swam slowly across to the steps, rose without coyness, without shame, no longer embarrassed by her small breasts and narrow hips, the lack of voluptuous womanliness in her figure. Noiselessly as a creature of the night, Blaize came towards her as she ran her hands through her hair, squeezing the water from the thick curls, pushing her fingers through them to drag the clinging locks back.

The moon shone full on his face, accenting the angular jaw, the striking planes and lines, and the stark, uncompromisingly masculine force and beauty. His eyes were too shadowed to see what he was thinking, but his stance, the waiting stillness as he watched, told her that she had his total, unblinking attention.

She walked slowly up the steps, unaware of anything but the potent masculinity in him, the way his clothes clung lovingly to the wide chest and shoulders, hugged the flat stomach and long, lean thighs. Strange sensations moved like needles of fire through her, filling her with an unutterable sense of rightness. This was meant to be. Tomorrow she might well regret what was about to happen, but for now she would take what the night offered, and there would be no holding back, no coy pretence. Regal as a queen, glowing with a ripe, eager sensuality, she went towards him, a small involuntary smile pulling at her mouth.

He stood with hands clenched at his sides and watched her come all the way up to him, her tall slenderness silvered by the moon, its vagrant light picking out the small, high breasts, the feminine curve of her waist and the sleek length of her legs, the delicate, feminine bones, strong yet with a grace that was wholly, unconsciously hers.

His eyes burned over her body, lighting conflagrations wherever they touched. In a moment of insight she thought that he was bringing her to bloom, ripening deep-seated hungers she had never experienced before. Like a flower at its most perfect moment she was sweetly erotic with the need for satisfaction.

She stopped just a few inches away and said his name, looking up into the austere, terrible face of a judge, a man without mercy.

'Oriel,' he said deeply. He touched her mouth, then his hand curved around the back of her neck and he pulled her gently into his body.

He was hot, and every muscle was tense with restraint; she gave a funny little shudder. Her body, her instincts were telling her that he wanted her, yet some part of her warned of peril beyond imagining. She stared into silver eyes that were glittering with nameless emotions, and then he kissed her mouth, and she was lost to a wild onslaught of desire.

Her hands fastened on to his shoulders as she surrendered, opening at last her heart as well as her body to his passion, free from the inhibitions that had kept her from offering herself to any other man. She knew that he wanted her; she was no longer ashamed of her body. With a woman's pride she gave him everything she had.

And he took. His mouth burned into hers, hard and fierce. This was not the time for tenderness; that would come later. For now there was this hunger that had been repressed all her life to be assuaged in the fires of his need. She shuddered, and he hauled her close, closer, warming her against the heat of his body, his arms like steel bands across her back, imprisoning her in a cage fashioned by desire.

He touched his mouth to the rapid, painful pulse in her throat, and she felt his heart beating like the time pattern of the universe, beating for her.

Her breath stopped as his hand found the small globe of her breast; she groaned, and his mouth swooped, and touched the peaking nipple, encompassed it, drew it inside the dark warmth and began a rhythmic suckling that sent sharp arrows of sensation to pierce her, shooting through nerve impulses to conjoin in the apex of her body, a sweet pain, a gathering storm, dark, mindless tides of hunger reducing her to unthinking bliss, a total dependence on his hands, his mouth, the dominating strength of his body.

She thought dazedly, Now I know why—know how——

He lifted his head and she opened her eyes in protest, the sleepy droop of her lashes heavy against her cheekbones. His hand slid from her breast, down the narrow waist, and on down.

In an impeded voice he said, 'You look like a nixie. Do you know what a nixie was, Oriel? She was a water nymph, beautiful and desirable, and she lay in wait for men. She desired them, and any man would do. But it was dangerous to lie with a nixie, because after a man had made love to one he lost all desire for mortal women. And the nixie was never faithful; once she'd slept with a mortal she no longer wanted him.'

She made a slow sound of protest as his hand stroked over her hip, found the warm tangle between her legs, and slid home.

'Is this for me?' he asked harshly. 'Or is it for André Hunter? Did you make love with him in your room, Oriel, or didn't you have time, and are you using for me the desire that he roused?'

Sheer shock robbed her of words. She stared at him, seeing the twist to his mouth, the silver steel of his gaze, feeling at the same time the smooth intrusion of his fingers in her body. Shame, more intense than any other emotion, spread like a black flood through her. She pushed at him with all her might, but he was as solid and immovable as eternity.

Then she tried to pull away, but his hands came up to fasten on to her upper arms. There was no cruelty in his grip, but she felt the dark impulse to it beating against her.

He was smiling, coldly, without mercy or respect. 'I'm quite prepared to indulge this—itch,' he said offensively, 'but I want you to realise that I am not so easily manipulated as perhaps you thought.'

She welcomed the anger. It at least gave her some pride, held the darkness at bay for a little while. 'You are foul,' she said, her voice cold as the moonlight, all colour fled.

'Realistic. He was, after all, in your bedroom.'

'For a few minutes.'

His brows lifted, but his voice was even, almost reflective as he said, 'Quite a while, I believe. At least two people attested to that. Ah, didn't you realise that there had been eyes watching your little idyll out here? Not unkind eyes, merely a little concerned, because André is rather notorious. He found you very attractive, he was making no bones about it. With André, to think is to act. He's a fast worker.'

In a voice sweet and limpid and cold as a mountain stream she said, 'He and I talked out here for a short time, and on the way back in I wrenched my ankle again. He helped me up to my room, got a cold cloth for it, then left. He was kind and helpful and not at all amorous.'

'Yet I stood, in the best traditions of high farce, like a jealous lover and watched him walk down the stairs with the satisfied smile of a man who has achieved what he wants. And when you walked across to me a few minutes ago, there was no sign of a limp.'

She looked at him, her heart slowing as she realised that he was not going to listen to her, he had made up his mind and she was convicted by a jury without mercy, without recourse.

'If you believe that,' she said, 'why did you kiss me just now?'

His mouth twisted in mockery, in cold, contemptuous irony. 'I made no overtures,' he reminded her. 'You came to me. And I am as weak as André. You are beautiful, and I wanted you. I still want you.'

He took her hand and dragged it down his body, showing her just how much he did want her. She made a quick gagging sound and wrenched her hand free as if the touch of his hardened flesh had burned her, and stepped back, saying harshly, 'You're despicable! I'll go tomorrow.'

'You signed a contract.' His voice was icily remote.

Shivering, she looked around the silver, sweet-scented night, searching for her nightgown, desperate to get away from him. Then the import of his words struck her. A cold wind touched her skin. 'But—you can't——'

'I can do anything,' he said, his voice calm and reflective as he watched her. 'I think perhaps you don't realise just how much I can do, Oriel. I can make it impossible for you to ever find another job. I can make your life so uncomfortable in so many ways that you might feel it necessary to flee the country. I can make it impossible for you to get a seat on any airline. I can call in favours and have you declared a prohibited immigrant in almost any country in the world. I can persuade the police to take a stifling interest in your behaviour. And if you try to run away, I can follow you to the ends of the earth and make your life a misery.'

'How can you do that? I've done nothing...'

He smiled again. 'You need a few lessons in the re-
alities of life,' he said calmly. 'I'm a powerful man, Oriel.
You'd probably be surprised at just how powerful I am.
I don't boast, and I don't make threats I can't carry
out.'

His voice was cool and dispassionate, but the blade
had been unsheathed, swift and clean and deadly, and
it was pointed at her heart. She had known he was
dangerous, but in her stupidity it had never occurred
that this was the sort of danger she had to fear.

Her eyes dilated in feral pain; she shuddered, her soul
accepting defeat. As she turned blindly, her foot slipped
and she fell into the water, the shock of its splash cutting
off the breath she tried to draw.

She felt the coping graze her head as she went in.
Perhaps she hit the bottom; she remembered very little
about the next few minutes, except that she was choking
and limp when strong arms hauled her out of the water,
and Blaize's heart beat heavily against her as he carried
her on to the lounger and put her down. Her chest hurt;
she coughed, and spat out water, and began to shiver,
long, slow shudders racking her body.

'I'll get you a towel,' he said harshly.

He rubbed her dry, ignoring her attempts to do it
herself, and put her nightgown on her, only then
stripping off with unselfconscious ease and drying
himself before pulling on a heavy towelling robe.

'Come on,' he said. 'Do you want me to carry you
in?'

She flinched away. Something ugly moved in his eyes,
then was gone. 'Right,' he said unemotionally. 'Get
going.'

He made her shower, threatening to stand in the
bathroom with her until she promised that she would do
it, then left to change out of his robe. Numbly, almost
successfully shutting off the hideous clamour in her

mind, she let the warm water play over her shaking body until he tapped on the door and said something. Her breath caught in a harsh sob, but she turned the water off. If she didn't get out he was quite likely to come in, and she thought she would die if he saw her naked again.

With hands that shook she dried herself and pulled on a pair of thin cotton pyjamas. Avoiding her eyes in the mirror, she combed her hair. For a second only her hands clenched on to the side of the vanity bench, the knuckles showing white as she closed her eyes and took a deep breath. Then she went into the bedroom, the last remnants of her pride blanking out all expression from her still white face.

Blaize was standing by the bed, looking down at the rumpled blankets, his profile a knife slash against the soft blues and greys of the curtains. A muscle flicked in the arrogant line of his jaw, and his mouth was a thin, cruel line. He had changed into black trousers and a thin black shirt and was waiting impassively, big and dominating, a lethal prowler in the jungle of the night, his whole stance indicating antagonism.

'Brandy,' he said, putting a glass in her hand. 'Drink it.'

She bit her lip, but tossed the brandy down, welcoming the ferocious bite of the spirit. Bruised and battered by her emotions, her whole being in tormented disarray, she thought that the last incident had reduced everything that had happened that night to farce of the broadest sort. Still, at least it had anaesthetised her feelings.

'Into bed,' he ordered.

She looked at her tossed bed, and said without any apprehension of being believed. 'We didn't make love, Blaize.'

'It doesn't matter,' he said indifferently. 'I overreacted. However, it doesn't alter the basic premise, which is that you have signed a contract, and I have no intention of letting you walk out on it. Your love-affairs take second place to Sarah's welfare.'

He was gone the next morning, he and James Weatherall, and Oriel welcomed the three weeks until he came back with gratitude. It gave her time to accept the fact that she loved him, and that he felt nothing so basic for her.

It gave her time to develop a shell to hide her broken heart from probing eyes.

It gave her time to settle into the big house against one of Auckland's volcanic cones, fit into the routine, and establish friendly relations with the housekeeper and the gardener, who was also the chauffeur when one was needed. It gave her time to discover that pain was a constant that took away her appetite and her sleep, that ached from her soul to her heart, colouring her whole world grey.

It gave her time to learn that she could spend all night awake, and function more or less normally the next day.

And it gave her time to become accustomed to the fact that her mother had decided to emigrate to the warmer climate and bigger pool of Australia. Offered a new position as head of a famous modelling agency in Brisbane, she came back only to work out her time and pack up. So excited was she by her new life that she could spare no more than a very cursory interest in Oriel's, for which her daughter was profoundly grateful.

She and Jo might never been very close, but it was a wrench to wave her off, knowing she would only come back for holidays.

No sooner was Jo gone than Blaize returned to enrol Sarah at a private school with an excellent reputation and small classes. It was purgatory to go with him, especially when both the registrar and the headmistress mistook her for his wife and she had to endure his firm correction of them both. But then Oriel discovered that she could endure almost anything, except the signs of tiredness Blaize bore, and the fact that his eyes were hooded and calm when they met hers.

It was all over. Whatever he had felt for her he had managed to kill. While he was away she had toyed with the idea of forcing him to listen to her, but one glance into those weary, implacable eyes had convinced her that if she tried, she would only be exposing herself to more humiliation. For some reason he had decided that he did not need to want her, and so he had used his considerable will to kill the emotions she had roused in him.

She wished it was so easy for her.

Amazingly, it was possible to live a normal life, to seem perfectly sane and rational, when her whole being ached with an intolerable pain. It wasn't pleasant, but it was possible.

Just as it was possible to know that Blaize was with another woman and betray nothing. He rarely spent the evenings at home. Oriel's pain was almost physical, a shaft of burning agony, but she concealed it.

They inhabited the same house, they loved the same children; sometimes when Simon was on leave from school they took them out together, for all the world like a family. They were polite and distant to each other, warm and loving with the children.

And Oriel told herself that it was worth it. It had to be worth it. Certainly the children bloomed. Sarah lost the worried look that had seemed permanent for her, and with the rapid growth of her teeth, and the equally rapid increase in her reading ability, she became the happy, loving child she had been intended to be.

And Simon said several times, very casually, that he enjoyed coming home for leave at weekends now.

About halfway through her period of probation Oriel decided that she was not going to eat her heart out any more. On her deathbed she would remember Blaize, but she was not going to look back on a life blighted by a lost love. If she never loved again, never married, never held her own child to her heart, she would grieve, but she would not let it ruin her life; she was going to live fully and well.

The decision marked some kind of turning-point. When consulted, Blaize agreed to her plans, with the proviso that the children, especially Sarah, must come first.

'Of course,' Oriel said simply.

'Does this mean that you aren't thinking of leaving us when the three months are up?' he drawled lazily.

She shook her head. 'I don't know,' she said, retreating, not yet ready to admit that it was impossible for her to leave Sarah.

He gave her a mocking smile. For a moment she hesitated. It was the first crack in the meticulous courtesy he had been treating her to. Then she met his eyes, cold, polished pewter, and gave up the idea.

So she enrolled at university for a degree course in education. At least the tuition fees were not a burden. She was being paid ridiculously well for a job that involved very little work. The housekeeper did all the housewifely things, and it was very easy to love Sarah.

And then André Hunter reappeared on the scene. And Oriel found that the weeks of self-restraint had been for nothing, because she wanted nothing more than to tear his eyes out for being the cause of all her wretchedness.

It was irrational and unfair, because she knew perfectly well that he was not the reason for Blaize's rejection of her. No doubt, she had decided on too many of her sleepless nights, Blaize had realised that he did not really want a tall, thin, awkward woman, and had merely used his well-known aversion to sharing as an easy excuse for his decision.

So when André Hunter came strolling up to her as she walked out on to the street from the university one perfect autumn day, she looked at him with the first signs of spirit she had evinced since the night of the party, her eyes far from sleepy.

A wicked, mocking smile touched the knowing mouth. 'Ouch!' he complained. 'All right, what have I done?'

She had regained control. 'Nothing,' she said calmly. 'Why are you here?'

'Oh, the university held a lunch for various people, and invited me. It was dull, but I'm glad now I came. When I woke this morning I looked out of the window and told myself that such a day had to have something exceedingly pleasant in wait for me. Come and have a drink.'

She didn't want to, but even as she shook her head he took her arm and coaxed, 'I promise I won't try to seduce you in the bar. In spite of what you read in the gossip columns, you're not automatically branded a scarlet woman if you go to a pub with me once or twice.'

A smile trembled on her mouth. André pressed home his advantage. 'Besides, I want to know more about you. I like you, which is an odd reaction for me to have. Perhaps it's because you are head over heels in love with your boss, so I'm in no danger.'

'I don't——' To her horror her eyes filled with tears.

He clicked his fingers and a car rolled up. 'One of my few extravagances,' he said as he opened the back door for her. He gave the driver some instructions and then turned back to her as the car rolled regally down the road. 'Sorry,' he said, clearly sincere. 'I'm an idiot.'

'I'm the idiot.' She blew her nose and sat up straight. 'I don't usually burst into tears, I promise you.'

'I'm sure you don't. How's the foot?'

'Oh, it's fine, no problems.'

His green gaze never left her face. 'No more swelling in the afternoon?'

'No, it's completely better.'

He leaned back against the opulent leather and began to talk, cheerfully, idly, with a stinging wit that amused her and an oddly gentle attitude that surprised her. She was even more surprised when she realised that instead of going to a hotel or café they were being driven through one of the leafy suburbs. 'I don't——' she began, frowning.

'Relax,' André ordered cheerfully, patting her hand in a most avuncular manner. 'I thought you'd prefer to have your drink in privacy.'

She eyed him carefully. He was smiling, but she saw nothing but a warm concern that insensibly comforted her. Instinctively she knew she had nothing to fear from him, whatever his reputation with women. And why shouldn't she go? she thought on a burst of defiance directed at Blaize. Sarah wasn't due to be picked up for another hour and a half.

He had been watching her carefully, for he gave a wicked chuckle, green eyes gleaming with mischief. 'That's the girl,' he encouraged softly. 'I knew that a woman with a smile like yours wasn't the sort to listen to vulgar gossip. Or allow herself to be intimidated by a man who doesn't know when he's hit the jackpot.'

'How——?' She bit her lip.

'Because,' he said easily, leaning back and surveying the back of the driver's head with a calm amusement she found irritating, 'he was watching you like a hawk the night of the party, and he did not like it when he saw us together. Naturally he would warn you against me. After all, he warned me off in the most threatening way.' He ignored her gasp, and went on meditatively, 'Of course I took note. It's not considered healthy to oppose Blaize Stephenson, and the man is known for his dislike of sharing anything—especially his women. Witness my restraint these past weeks. However, it has become common knowledge among those who need to know these things that he's not in the best of humours. Normally he spends a lot of time overseas, but this year everything is being done from home. And very many people have felt the lash of the great man's tongue. Poor old James Weatherall is looking distinctly harassed. Why? we ask ourselves. It can't be lack of feminine company, because he has been seen out with other beautiful, accommodating damsels.'

She flinched and he patted her hand again, a little less avuncularly this time. Carefully she folded both hers in her lap, composing her face into an expressionless mask.

'But dog in the manger has never been Blaize's way,' he mused, smiling, slanting her a very perceptive glance.

She said nothing, wishing heartily that she hadn't given in to that most uncharacteristic burst of defiance. In spite of herself she liked André, but he was altogether too sharp, and she had a sinking feeling that he hadn't brought her here to give her a drink and a little social chit-chat.

A few minutes later the car turned in through massive gates to a tall apartment building, one of the few allowed some years ago before zoning restrictions became more rigid.

The driver put them tenderly out and they walked in through the security doors and across the entrance to the lifts. Another couple were there; to her astonishment Oriel recognised the Duncans, Matt and Lora. His hand at her back, André acknowledged their greetings. Oriel felt colour surge into her cheeks at Lora's surprised look, and the cool, somewhat assessing glance Matt Duncan gave her.

They were perfectly affable, however, Lora informing her that they had come down for an exhibition of French Impressionists in the art gallery.

'We must get together,' she finished with the friendliness Oriel liked so much.

'I'd like that,' said Oriel.

'It can't be tonight, we're going out tonight. Tomorrow?' Lora directed an enquiring glance at her husband. He nodded. 'How about lunch tomorrow?'

'No, I'm sorry, the children and I are flying up to the Bay this afternoon, to spend Easter there.'

Lora's disappointed look vanished. 'Oh, well, we might see you up there, then.'

'I'll look forward to it,' Oriel said, realising with something of a start that she was.

'Speaking of looking forward,' André said outrageously, 'we'd better go, Oriel.' Nodding to Matt, he bent and kissed Lora's hand, ignoring the troubled look she gave him, and swept Oriel inexorably towards the lift, barely allowing her time to say her goodbyes.

Once inside the lift he collapsed against the wall, saying wearily, 'No, don't splutter at me, Oriel——'

'Why did you say that? You deliberately made it sound as though—as though——'

'As though we were having an assignation? Of course I did. I have to live up to my reputation, you know.'

'Not at the expense of mine!'

He had opened his eyes and fixed her with a gleaming glance. 'Dearest girl, the minute you moved in with Blaize your reputation was shot. Especially when everyone saw how he watched you the night of the party.'

The lift stopped. She said, 'I don't want to come in.'

'Of course you do.' He took her hand, surprising her with his strength as he urged her out into a hallway. 'Does it matter, Oriel? You know perfectly well that I'm not going to leap on you, and if what I said was offensive,

I apologise. Not that you need to worry, because neither of the Duncans gossip.'

Unwillingly, nagged by an aching sense that he was up to something, that she was being incredibly foolish, she let him persuade her into his apartment.

He gave her coffee, made her laugh, showed her just how charming he could be and then took her home, delivering her just in time for her to go and pick Sarah up from school.

So much for her inchoate fears! Admittedly, his eyes gleamed with something close to mockery, but he couldn't have been more pleasant or less threatening.

Both children were bubbling with excitement at the prospect of six days spent at the Bay, preceded by the delights of a flight in the small plane that would take them to the airport at Kerikeri. Not at all eager to revisit the scene of her humiliation, Oriel listened with a wry smile as the chauffeur took them out to the airport in time to catch the six o'clock plane.

It was dusk when they reached Kerikeri, darkness falling properly as Ned drove them around the southern shores of the Bay to the station, on the way pointing out the massive pillars that denoted the entrance to Matt Duncan's station, Kahurangi.

Allowing herself only a small, wistfully envious thought of the couple, so much in love that they seemed irradiated with it, Oriel wondered whether the function they were attending that night was the same as the one that Blaize was going to.

She had no idea what it was; she'd never asked, and he'd never said—their conversation was mainly about the children, but he had told her that he wouldn't be able to come up that night because he had to go out. She thought bleakly of the exquisite creature who had come to the house one Sunday afternoon; was he out with her?

Not that she had stayed long. Blaize had seen her in the office and she had left within twenty minutes. It was, however, long enough for Oriel to learn to hate her.

'Nearly there,' she said a few minutes later, as the car turned off the shockingly bad metal road on to the much better surface of the long drive in.

Sarah hugged herself gleefully. 'Can we go for a swim?'

'Not tonight, sweetheart.' Firmly banishing the images that that brought to mind, Oriel looked pensively at the dark shapes of the hills. Somewhere in there she had stumbled and staggered on her way to the beach, and to Blaize.

Instinct should have directed her elsewhere. No, she thought suddenly and passionately, she was glad. At least she knew now what it was like to love, totally, completely, with all her heart and soul. She would not have wanted a calmer, less painful life.

It was quite cool when they finally got in, cold enough for Sarah to give up without complaint any idea of swimming. Kathy greeted them with pleasure and dinner, exclaiming over Sarah's new teeth, and how much Simon had grown, so it was later than usual when they went to bed, but by ten-thirty both children were asleep, and Oriel was yawning herself. She had a long bath and was in bed and asleep by midnight.

It was the noise of the launch engines that woke her. As she rolled over in her bed she checked the clock. Two o'clock! She leapt out of bed and ran quietly down to the conservatory, peering out into the brilliant moonlight. A red glow startled the darkness, then was dowsed. She heard a soft male voice, and realised that no one was stealing the launch; it was coming in. Curiosity held her still. Had Ned been indulging in a little night fishing? But he wouldn't take the launch, he had his own runabout.

Then a lithe silhouette swung on to the jetty, and her hand stole up to her heart. Blaize had arrived! He must have flown up and been collected by Ned in the launch. It was a much shorter distance by sea and took only about the same time as by road.

Quickly, moving as quietly as she could, she raced back to her room and was in bed when she heard the unmistakable sounds of someone moving softly through the house. Insensibly she relaxed. So it made it all the more shattering when the door was flung open, the light switched on, and in a voice that for all its softness flayed the skin from her bones Blaize demanded, 'What the hell were you doing in André Hunter's apartment yesterday?'

CHAPTER NINE

ORIEL gaped at Blaize, her eyes wide with confusion as she took in the dangerous tautness of his stance, the anger blazing in his expression. Then anguish at the long weeks of insulting politeness burst through in a flood of fury so intense it took her a moment to be able to speak, and when she did it was in a voice that trembled with rage.

'How dare you?' she exploded, jerking upright. 'Get out of here!'

He came in silently, powerful and smooth as the death lunge of a predator. 'If you want an affair,' he said between his teeth, 'then by God, Oriel, you can have one with me. You don't have to go to bloody André Hunter to satisfy your urges.'

Temper dilated her eyes into pools of darkness. 'With you?' she spat. 'Why would I want to go to bed with a man who rejected me as cruelly as he could, who let me offer myself to him and then turned me down with a few scathing comments about my lack of suitability? Tell me, why the hell would I be stupid enough to give you another chance?'

He hauled her out of the bed in one swift movement, all control gone now, his lean hands ferocious as they shook her. 'Because at least I love you, damn you!' he snarled.

Adrenalin was surging through her body, wiping away all restraint. 'Love me?' she hooted, her laughter as savage as her anger. 'You don't know how to love anyone, unless it's a child. Loving someone means that you want them to be happy. You've done your best to make sure I'm as unhappy as I can possibly be, you swine. And now, just because your territorial instinct is roused, you've decided you do want me after all. André said you weren't a dog in the manger. He was wrong.'

His hands tightened cruelly on the delicate bones of her shoulders. She cried out, and he released her, his face white, his mouth tightly compressed as he fought for control. 'I'm sorry,' he said, pushing back the thin material of her pyjamas to look bleakly at the marks he had made. He closed his eyes for a second, then opened them and bent and kissed the maltreated skin. His lips were cold, and suddenly her righteous rage ebbed and died, leaving the taste of ashes in her mouth.

'It doesn't matter,' she said wearily. 'It doesn't matter, Blaize. Just leave me alone. Please.'

'I can't.' He lifted his head and looked into her eyes, his own shadowed and driven. After a haunted second her repeated softly, 'I can't, darling. I tried, God knows I tried. I know you're not ready for this. But when I heard that you'd been seen in Hunter's apartment——'

'The Duncans.'

'Yes. Lora didn't want to tell me, she felt a heel, but she was worried, and she knows how I feel about you.'

'And how do you feel about me?' she asked very steadily.

'I love you.'

Oh, how she wanted to believe him. But she loved him so much that she couldn't accept anything less than a like commitment from him; it was ominous that there had been no mention of love until he thought she was having an affair with André. Was it his masculine possessiveness, the trait that refused to let him share, that had produced this sudden change?

'I don't believe you,' she said sadly.

'You will.' He saw that she was trembling and said, 'I shouldn't have come in here, you're exhausted, but when I heard Lora say you'd been with Hunter I wanted to kill you and him and myself for being so stupidly, wilfully blind to the most important thing that has ever happened to me. Darling, sit down. It's cold, pull the blankets around you.'

She stared at him, obeying dazedly as he urged her down on to the bed and dragged the duvet around her so that she was cocooned in it. When she was comfortable he sat down on the end of the bed and looked at her, his eyes travelling over her pale face, his mouth tilted in the faint, ironic smile that had been missing these last weeks.

Very softly, he said, 'When I came across you on the beach in the storm, wet and muddy, pale blue and shivering, a drowned rat personified, I thought you were plain, a lanky creature with a forgettable face. Then you began to dry out, and you had skin as clear and warm as the palest silk, and that wild hair started to curl around your face. You looked like a gypsy, untamed and irresistible, your smoky blue eyes long and slanted and lazy, summoning me to a feast you had never attended yourself. I was fascinated, I didn't know that innocence and carnality could be combined so invitingly in one graceful girl. I wanted to indulge the carnality and take the innocence. I wanted to sink my hands into that incredible hair, hold your face still while I took your mouth. I wanted to feel you against me, beneath me, on me, all around me, your mouth on my skin, your body against mine. But you were innocent, and I knew I had to leave you alone.'

'You couldn't know that,' she whispered, his words melting some deep, frozen part of her. 'I don't wear my virginity like a flag.'

He laughed deep in his throat. 'That's exactly what you do, my darling. And if I hadn't known before, I'd have been convinced of your lack of experience when I kissed you that first time. The day you'd been swimming.'

She shivered, remembering the weird atmosphere of that day, the heavy mist pressing on to them, the wild passion he had aroused in her.

'Yes,' he said, watching the expressions chase across her face. 'It was like nothing else I had ever experienced. I had never felt such an intensity of emotion, such need, and you were only too clearly caught up in the same web. But it was equally clear that you didn't know what the hell was happening to you. So I backed off.'

'I thought you were wooing me a little because you wanted me to work for you, to be a mother for Sarah.'

His mouth twisted sardonically. 'Yes. Just a few kisses, I told myself, they can't do any harm, and if she's weak enough to fall for that kind of sensual blackmail—well, what is it to me? It's all in a good cause. Oh, I wanted you right from the start. It was only too damned obvious. Normally I don't harass women who say they don't want me to touch them. I've always prided myself on my self-control, yet I couldn't keep my hands off you! But I wasn't prepared to admit that I could fall in love after one look.'

Her eyes were very clear as she said, 'You can't really. It's not possible.'

'Is that what you told yourself?' His smile was a masterpiece of irony. 'What did happen, then? You sat up in bed, clean and pink after your shower, and stole my heart away.'

'I couldn't believe it,' she whispered. 'Your eyes turned from pewter to silver, and they set me on fire. I honestly thought for a moment I'd had an electric shock.'

'You too?' He leaned forward so that he could reach her hair, threading through a curl, straightening it, pulling it out, then releasing it back into the tight ringlet. His mouth compressed. 'But, beloved, we didn't just fall in love. You claimed me, and I knew that I possessed you. All within half an hour of setting eyes on each other.'

'Then what took us so long?'

He sat back with an air of tense resolution, his features angular and drawn. 'An arrogant refusal to admit that I am as human as the next man. I hadn't believed in love for so long that I denied it when it came. And kept on denying it until I realised just how stupid I was being.'

'Why? What made you so adamant that it was just "nature's way of perpetuating genes"?'

'Cynicism,' he said gravely. 'And pride. Cynicism because there are always women who are willing to sell themselves.'

'Men do it too.'

He nodded, his mouth twisting, seemingly absorbed in what his fingers were doing to her hair. 'Yes, I know. I became accustomed to them, Oriel, those men and women who want money or power so badly they're prepared to sell their bodies or their principles for either or both. I forgot the multitudes of people who try to keep to their high standards. I've always prided myself on my principles, but along the way I lost my ideals.'

'And pride? You said it was cynicism and pride.'

'Ah, pride. I'd come to think that love was for lesser people. Blaize Stephenson saw more clearly; he was in control. Then I saw you and I was forced to admit that the only reason for my vaunted self-possession was that I hadn't yet met you. I felt—a lesser person, I suppose.' His smile was narrow, echoing the self-contempt in his tone. 'Less of a man, because I was at your mercy. So fear came into it too. I was afraid that by loving you I was losing myself. It wouldn't have been so bad if it hadn't been so overpowering, so primitively basic. I looked at you and everything, the intelligence I had always been so proud of, my will-power, my strength, was swamped in a deluge of emotion.'

'It happened to me too,' she admitted, moved by his brutal frankness. 'It still scares me. It's so—so mindless, a kind of blind hunger. I thought it was a violent attraction, a kind of irritation of the senses.' Smiling, she told him about the debate she had had with herself on the beach about pheromones. 'I felt as though you'd cast some kind of spell over me, and I couldn't struggle free of it.'

His hand touched hers. She shivered, and he said hopelessly, 'If this is love I don't know how people cope with it. It eats away at me—I thought love was supposed to be happy, to make the world a more pleasant place. Instead it's terrifying, not the cosy, safe emotion I'd always imagined it to be, but dangerous, and exciting, and addictive. But as well as that—*claiming*, there was your kindness, your gentleness—your honesty. What I feel for you is so much more than this damned uncomfortable desire.'

She caught his hand and pulled it to her lips. 'I love you, Blaize. I want to make love with you, I want to live with you and have your children, I want to be there for you for the rest of my life. Perhaps this kind of love will change—after all, we'll change over the years, but although the thought of spending the rest of my life with you frightens me as much as it thrills me, I want to.'

'Dearest heart.' His voice was incredibly moved, thick with emotion. His hand tightened about her face, then lifted to thread into her hair. Pulling her face towards him so that his breath warmed her mouth, he said very deep and low, 'I want all that too. To walk into a room and know that your eyes light up only for me, to know that you are there, always to be there for you. And at night, to go with you up to our bedroom and watch you undress, to be able to touch you, and at last to lose myself in you—Oriel, I want that so much. I've been eaten away with hunger, these weeks with you, so calm, so aloof, in my house. Even before I heard about your visit to Hunter I'd decided that I wasn't going to last out, that my pride was an arrogant desire to punish you and myself because I was afraid of being vulnerable.'

'What were you going to do?'

He moved down the bed and loosened the duvet, pulling her gently against him, as he smoothed her hair back from her suddenly hot cheek. 'I was going to wait until we were alone here and ask if there was any possibility that we might start over again.' Grim laughter was an undertone in the deep voice. 'I was going to tell you that I loved you, and that my soul was dying without you. What would you have said, Oriel?'

She listened to his heartbeat, watched with sultry eyes the pulse in the strong brown column of his throat. 'I'd probably have told you to go to hell,' she said demurely.

His teeth gleamed a moment as he laughed. 'Then perhaps it's just as well Lora spilled the beans, and I came up here seething with righteous anger. How long would you have made me plead?'

'I couldn't make you plead!'

'Oh, yes,' he said calmly. 'Didn't you know, my heart's delight, my lovely lady? You could make me plead, and enjoy doing it. Why do you think I've been fighting you for so long?'

She looked directly at him. He was watching her, that little smile at the corners of his mouth, but in his eyes was the naked truth. 'I would never make you plead,' she said steadily. 'Pleading has no place between lovers.'

'My compassionate love. Then are we going to wait?'

Oriel knew what he meant. His voice stroked along her nerves, teasing each cell in her body into life. She lifted heavy lashes and smiled at him, pierced through by his smile, his narrowed, brilliant glance. 'No,' she whispered. 'Why should we wait? I love you. You love me. Isn't that all that's necessary?'

He carried her up the stairs and into his bedroom, his arms strong and sure about her, havens when she needed them. As he stood her beside the huge bed he asked on a note of passionate laughter, 'Are you shy?'

Colour flaked the length of her cheekbones. 'Yes. I suppose I'm still terrified that you—that you might find me—too thin.'

His brows drew together. 'Your mother may not have recognised your potential,' he said curtly, 'but I happen to like tall women with bodies like racehorses, lithe and long-limbed, with silky skin and——'

'Small breasts,' she said, pulling his hand to cover the swell of her breast. His fingers cupped, moved slowly, silkily across the taut, expectant tips. She shivered at the uncomfortable excitement of her nipples peaking.

'Small,' he said on a sigh. 'My heart, they fit my hand perfectly. And we know they fit my mouth perfectly. They will fit the mouths of our children perfectly. How can they be too small? By the time I've finished loving you, you will know that they are perfect, that you are perfect, made for me, made for my loving, made for my life and my heart.'

Sensation sizzled through her. She had never known that knees could literally go weak and useless at the words of another, but hers weren't able to support her. Sinking against him, she held up her mouth. His came down to meet its innocent invitation, gently at first, and then, at her ardent, untrammelled response, with a ferocity that should have frightened the wits out of her.

Perhaps it did, for her wits certainly left her. Recklessly, blindly, she offered the bounty of her body, shuddering with delight as his trembling hands wrenched her clothes from her until she was naked before him, her body open to his gaze.

'You look like a goddess,' he said, his voice impeded yet ringing with the control he was exerting. 'Not full-breasted Juno, but Diana, the huntress, strong and graceful and lithe, so dangerous that no man could look at her and survive. Oriel, for the only time in my life since the very first, I'm terrified that I'm going to do something wrong. I need you so much... I'm afraid I'll hurt you, disgust you...'

'Nothing you could do could disgust me,' she whispered, her hands sliding up to undo the buttons on his shirt. 'And if something goes wrong—well, what does it matter? We have a lifetime to get it right, haven't we?'

'My lovely, sane darling!' He gave the triumphant laugh of a lover, and kissed her, holding her a long moment against his hard body. 'Yes. If I go too fast, it simply means that next time I'll be able to slow things down until you're screaming for fulfilment. Now, are you going to undress me, or shall I put a stop to the torture you're indulging in and yank my clothes off myself?'

His shirt gaped open, but she had got no further, her hands side-tracked into searching out the whorls and scrolls of hair that formed fine patterns across his chest. Her questing fingers found the tiny, hard nubs of his nipples; she put her mouth to them, but jerked her head away when he groaned.

'Don't you like it?' she asked worriedly.

'Yes.'

She understood. Smiling, she did it again, and slid her hands down to his belt. 'It won't come undone,' she whispered in frustration.

He wrenched it free, and stepped out of his trousers and the briefs beneath, bent to kiss her, easing her carefully into his embrace so that she became accustomed to his full arousal. Then she was lifted, and put in the bed, the sheet cool on her back; he hauled the bedclothes down and stood for a moment, his pale, glittering gaze tracing the contours of her body, the sweet curves and long limbs, the flushed skin.

'All spare, graceful beauty,' he murmured in a voice she barely heard. 'Clean, elegant lines with no need for an embarrassment of embellishment.'

All shyness gone, Oriel smiled and held up her arms to him. He was magnificent, she thought hazily, the splendid masculine presence never more wonderful than now, unclothed and revealed to her, all barriers gone.

He came down, that violent, devouring look on his face, but he was gentle even though his hands shook with the restraint he was imposing on himself, a restraint that made her angry in a vague way. Lost in the sensual daze she had fought so long, surrendering at last to the passion she had feared and avoided, she wanted him to feel the same release and freedom from constraint.

Something she had read in some magazine came to mind; with shy, untutored eagerness she began to copy what he was doing, her hands stroking over the magnificent body, finding the pleasure zones that made him groan deeply. His skin was smooth and warm and slightly damp, like magnificent living silk beneath her fingers, and she gloried in the shift and play of the muscles as he moved beside her.

All that power, she thought hazily as his mouth searched out the narrow indentation of her waist, the delicate hollow in the cradle of her hips, and yet when she touched him, when her mouth sought the hidden textures and tastes of him, he shuddered, completely at the mercy of the forces that linked them in this duet of passion.

But soon that kind of sensual play was not enough. His hand stroked slowly, leisurely across her flat stomach, down the silken length of her thighs, and moved, closer and closer to the aching centre of her body.

She held her breath, unable to control the involuntary thrust of her hips against that maddening, unfulfilling pressure.

'Wait,' he breathed. 'Ah, yes, Oriel, you want me...'

A streak of pure sensation ran through her. Taken by surprise, she arched and shuddered, biting her lips to hold back the cry wrenched from deep inside her.

'No,' he said, 'don't hide, don't keep it back. This is only true, it only means something, when we are honest and open, hiding nothing. Look, you can make me tremble, the touch of your hands can drive every thought from my mind but the need to take you. Don't hide from me, darling. I love you, I'll never abuse your trust.'

Shaken at the deep emotion in his words, she whispered like a vow, 'And I'll never abuse your trust, I swear. I love you——' A splintered cry broke from her lips. Helplessly her body arched again.

He made a low, feral sound, his eyes slits of molten silver as he moved over her. For a moment she held her breath. It was too late now to go back, instinct and passion had at last slipped the leash of that cool, clever brain. Sweat glistened on his big body, the muscles corded as he fought for control. Suddenly all her fears vanished. She smiled at him, love and trust combining with the smoky fumes of desire in a great sense of anticipation and welcome. His name shaped her lips, and eagerly she helped guide him as he took possession of all that she offered him.

For a moment he hesitated, his expression almost anguished. 'Oriel,' he groaned, 'I might hurt——'

'Darling, my love, my heart, please! Please, Blaize...'

She didn't know what she was pleading for, but he did, and after the slow, initial thrust that joined them he dragged air into his lungs, gritted his teeth and held her for long moments locked in his iron-bound grip while he fought for control again.

Oriel was transfixed, her body pierced with the sweet torment he had invoked, sensation racing through her in a tide as smooth as honey, as fierce as fire. She had expected pain, but there was none, merely a feeling of completion that still didn't satisfy her urgent, eager need.

When he began to establish a rhythm, a primitive dance of advance and retreat, she responded with a delighted, involuntary sensuality, moving her hips to hold him, discovering how to meet and match him, what movements made him gasp with pleasure.

Slowly, so slowly, her body reacted to his possession with rapture, a pleasure so intense that she thought she might die of it, yet every movement of his increased it, forcing her remorselessly, relentlessly, towards some unknowable peak, some pinnacle of ecstasy.

Her breath caught in her throat. Every muscle in her body strained, she wanted nothing more than to... than to... His eyes were fiercely compelling yet almost impersonal, as though he too was striving for that unknown destination.

She cried out his name, and waves of sensation began to build. Higher, higher, and then so high that she was no longer Oriel, he no longer Blaize; for uncountable moments they were a unity, racked with rapture, tormented by ecstasy, sundered from their previous existence by the shattering experience of that moment.

When she had come back down Oriel found that she was weeping; not sobbing, just tears running in tracks down her cheeks. Blaize had collapsed on her, his breathing painful as he dragged in air, his heartbeat blending with hers in wild cacophony. Sweat slicked their bodies; she lifted a hand, languid, boneless, and smoothed a lock of wet hair back from his brow.

'I'm too heavy,' he said.

'No.' She tightened herself around him, silken limbs, interior muscles she had never known she had keeping him imprisoned in her satin embrace.

'Yes.' He rolled over, his arms bringing her to rest on top of him.

She drooped her head on to his chest. 'If it's always like that,' she said faintly, 'we're going to have to ration ourselves. Too much of that and I'll die.'

His chest lifted on a silent laugh. 'You'll get used to it.'

'No. Never.'

'Yes. Did I hurt you?'

'No.' At his disbelieving look she sighed. 'A little pang at first, but that's all. You were very gentle.'

Again that ghost of a laugh. 'Thank heavens for that. I lost my head completely. Oriel?'

'Mmm?' She turned her head and nuzzled into his chest, lazily savouring the masculine scent, the erotically different textures of smooth skin and the fine hair above it.

'Was I mistaken or did you—did you climax?'

She smiled, a secret smile. 'If I didn't, I don't want to, ever. That's enough paradise for one soul to endure.'

He said quietly, 'I wonder if you have any idea how rare that is?'

'Yes. I read too, you know. Usually it takes a couple of years. But Blaize, it depends on trust, doesn't it? I trust you.'

His hand pressed her head into his chest. 'That's as wonderful as hearing that you love me.'

'They go together,' she said drowsily. 'Was it as good for you?'

She held her breath while he answered. He had made it wonderful for her, but she wanted it to be out of this world for him too.

He lifted her head. 'Look at me. No, don't go to sleep. Look at me.'

Slowly her lashes lifted. Her eyes were dark and hazy with the remnants of passion, his the silver of swords at dawn. 'It was magnificent,' he muttered. 'I have never been so—so lifted out of myself. I wish there were words to tell you.'

She said uncertainly, 'I was worried—I know experience is supposed to be—I mean, women improve with experience... And you...'

Her voice trailed away as he gave her a wicked, wholly masculine grin. 'I'm no virgin,' he said, 'but I'm not promiscuous either. Oh, in my youth, yes, I was just as lustful and thoughtless as any other, but I wasn't very old when I realised I needed more than a beautiful, willing body and a pleasant temperament. Since then I've had a couple of long-term relationships, which were amicably terminated, and that's all.'

'Then,' she said, returning his grin, 'you clearly have a great natural talent. I feel almost sorry that I'm not generous enough to share it with the rest of my sisters.'

He laughed at that, his narrowed eyes glinting with amusement and something else. To her amazement she found how swiftly she could recover from the shattering experience of a few minutes ago, and how easy it was to surrender again to the tides of passion he roused in her.

This time it was slow, a gentle rediscovery, a sweetness of wild honey flowing through her. His hands were magical instruments of pleasure, his mouth even more so, and she relearned the keen pleasure of kissing and caressing, that she could make his magnificent body shudder with need and pleasure, until at last they flowed together, male and female, perfectly complementary.

It was different, but the end was the same; total oblivion to everything but the immensity of rapture that rendered them unable to move, a tangle of limbs on the great bed.

She said in a shattered voice, 'I don't believe it.'

'Neither do I.' His voice was drowsy, yet permeated by a thoroughly male satisfaction. 'Do you know that we've done two impossible things?'

'Oh, that's easy when you're in love,' she said airily, still exalted by satisfaction and joy. 'What are they?'

'You reached your peak, and I made love to you twice in about twenty minutes.'

'Is it only twenty minutes...?' She lifted her head and looked at the bedside clock. 'Blaize! Blaize, it hasn't been twenty minutes! Some time during the night we must have been to sleep. It's morning! What about the children? Everybody will know what we've been doing!'

'A twenty-minute interval,' he said imperturbably, holding her still as she made desperate attempts to slide off the bed. His great strength kept her immobile as he said in a complacent voice, 'Haven't managed that since I was twenty-five or so.'

She laughed, kissing his mouth. 'I love you, but that doesn't mean I'll believe everything you say, my magnificent love. Blaize, we'll have to get up. Sarah's usually awake by six, and if I'm not in my bed she'll hurtle along here! I don't know how I'm going to meet anyone's eyes when I go down.'

'Perhaps you're the elixir of life,' he mused, not in the least concerned.

She choked, and put her arms around him, hugging all she could of him with her not inconsiderable strength. 'I love you.'

'And I love you. With all my heart. As far as the others are concerned, they'll all be only too pleased. Poor old James had borne the brunt of my temper—he'll be delighted. And the children will think it's a natural progression.' He must have felt the tiny stiffening of her body, because he pushed up her chin and looked into her eyes, his own very sharp. 'You're not still worried about that, are you?'

'I suppose—a little.'

He looked bleak. 'I suppose it's understandable.' She held her breath, then, as his finger touched her mouth, which was soft and bruised, she kissed it, and he said coolly, 'Well, how can I show you that I love you, that the fact you're so wonderful with the children is merely a delightful bonus? We've already tried the most obvious method——'

'You don't have to show me,' she said very tenderly. 'I believe you. After all, you trust me not to be marrying you for what you can give me, don't you? Trust is a two-way thing.'

'And you have an inferiority complex a mile high. Ah, well, it's something I'm going to enjoy whittling away. And yes, I do know you aren't marrying me for money.' He laughed and threaded his hands between her curls, holding her face still while he kissed her nose. 'You haven't got enough guile,' he teased.

She twisted a strand of curly chest-hair around her finger. 'Blaize, are you sure I can be a good wife to you? You lead such a different life——'

'I lead a very quiet life,' he said firmly. 'Except on very rare occasions I entertain business colleagues at lunch, so you won't have much to do with that side of my life, unless you want to. I have a small circle of close friends. You like the Duncans, don't you? They're a typical example. We socialise together, and very rarely do our names hit any of the gossip columns, either here or overseas. So if that's what's worrying you—forget it. My friends will like you, and more important, you will like them. They're informal and entertaining and pleasant. I'm more worried about whether you'll enjoy being my wife. I don't want you getting bored because you stay at home.'

She spread her fingers across his chest, feeling the steady beat of his heart, strong, reliable as the pulse of the universe. An upwelling of love drove the words from her brain.

'Oriel?' He sounded shaken, almost unsure of himself. 'I want you to be happy, darling.'

Now she looked at him, her lips trembling, her eyes blurred with tears. 'I can find plenty to do,' she said at last. 'I'll get my degree, and then I can teach adult reading courses, English as a first language—take fencing lessons! Don't worry about me, Blaize. I'm very adaptable.'

He snorted. 'You're about as adaptable as an iron bar, as I'm sure your mother would tell me. Why the tears?'

She told him, and that led to a very satisfactory interlude of soft kisses and low murmurs, until at last they got up. After some even more delightful minutes spent in the shower they emerged to find the children eating breakfast in the morning-room with a very smug Kathy.

Simon took one look at them and began to say something, then stopped. Without preamble Blaize informed them calmly, 'Oriel and I have decided to get married as soon as possible.'

There could be no doubt about the reception to this. Sarah danced up, clapping her hands, to hug them both, Simon gave a whoop and raced across to kiss Oriel clumsily on the cheek and, all dignity forgotten, hug Blaize. Kathy beamed and kissed them both and crowed, 'I knew it! I knew it! What took you so long?'

Blaize grinned. 'Stubbornness. Do you think you and James can arrange a wedding in a week?'

A ludicrous stare of dismay was rapidly replaced by calculation. 'Of course we can,' she said coolly. 'You watch!'

* * *

They managed it, but only just. Kathy bewailed the fact that the wedding cake didn't have time to mature, but she produced a wonderful light, summery spread for the twenty or so people who attended. The day before the ceremony Oriel's mother arrived in a private plane chartered by Blaize, accompanied by Oriel's two greatest friends, as well as David and his parents.

And Lora and Matt Duncan were to be there, Lora having rung as soon as she and Matt had come home to confess what she had done. Oriel had laughed, and had forgiven her when Lora had said, 'I was sure Blaize was in love with you, and I thought it was time someone showed him what he was risking by his stupidity. Matt told me I shouldn't interfere, and I've been so worried about it, wondering whether I did the right thing!'

'It was,' Oriel had assured her. She liked Lora, and had a premonition that she would come to like her even more in the years to come.

As Oriel had expected, her mother was astounded and a little aloof, as though she was irritated by what she persisted in calling 'Oriel's good luck'.

Blaize happened to overhear her, and said with crisp emphasis, 'More my good luck, I think.'

Jo replied a little self-consciously, 'Good luck for both of you, of course. So nice that Oriel gets on well with the children...'

Her voice died away at the sudden fire in her future son-in-law's eyes. He kissed Oriel's hand and said calmly, 'Unfortunately Oriel had this strange and totally untrue picture of herself as someone without charm, with nothing to offer a man. I won't have her upset or hurt in any way, and I can make life very uncomfortable for anyone who tries.'

Jo responded to the implied criticism and the almost naked threat with a gratifying fervour. 'I'm sure you can, and I hope you never have to do so. I wasn't trying to imply that you are only marrying her for her prowess with the children.' She met the implacable silver of his eyes with an appeasing smile. 'The idea is ridiculous! You could get a nurse for Sarah so easily. And I'm sure I only have to see you two together to understand how it is with you.'

'I'm sure you do,' he said with a cool politeness that gave Oriel the shivers.

Later, as they watched the dolphins leap around a yacht from the hill beside the Bay, he kissed her hair and said, 'All right now?'

'Yes.' She sighed and turned into his embrace, nestling close. 'My mother wasn't trying to make mischief, you know. It's just that she's always seen me as someone totally without attraction, so she honestly can't understand what you see in me.'

'Is she blind?'

'No.' She kissed his chin, and rubbed her forehead against the slightly rough silk of his jawline. 'She wanted a son, or failing that, a pretty little girl. I was wild, and tomboyish—Spider-legs, she used to call me. I just got stuck in that image. And even you, my dearest, very biased love, have to admit that I didn't grow into a pretty woman.'

'No, you're beautiful.' She laughed up at him, and he said seriously, 'I'll convince you of it if it's the last thing I do. When I look at you, you fill my eyes. You are perfect to me, everything that a woman should be. But even though I can't get enough of your beautiful body, even though I lose myself so completely in you, when I look at you it's not that I see. Or not entirely. It's the warmth and generosity of your spirit that shines through those delicious outward layers, the love you give so freely, the laughter and intelligence, the strength and the passion and the loyalty. I love you. That encompasses it all.'

Unbearably moved, she lifted sparkling eyes to him. 'I don't deserve that,' she whispered, 'but I'm going to try. And although I fell in love with you at first sight I really learned to love you when I realised how much you loved the children, how gentle you were with Sarah, how your strength and the power you wield so effortlessly were tempered by a generous spirit and a great kindness. I love you.'

The sun set in a blaze of crimson and scarlet and tangerine, but they didn't see it. Tomorrow was their wedding-day, the social sealing of their bond, but this was the final moment of the journey they had both begun when she had collapsed at his feet on this summer coast, exhausted by the pain and the storm but determined to reach the end of her journey if she had to crawl to get there.

Tomorrow they began another journey, longer and more difficult than any other, but they were supported by the knowledge they carried in their hearts, the conviction of love returned, the pledging of their efforts to make their life's journey one that they made together.

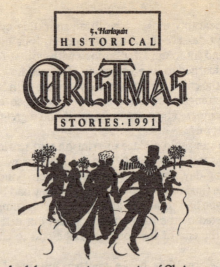

Harlequin HISTORICAL

CHRISTMAS

STORIES · 1991

Bring back heartwarming memories of Christmas past
with HISTORICAL CHRISTMAS STORIES 1991,
a collection of romantic stories
by three popular authors.
The perfect Christmas gift!

Don't miss these heartwarming stories,
available in November
wherever Harlequin books are sold:

CHRISTMAS YET TO COME
by Linda Trent
A SEASON OF JOY
by Caryn Cameron
FORTUNE'S GIFT
by DeLoras Scott

**Best Wishes and Season's Greetings
from Harlequin!**

HARLEQUIN

Romance

HARLEQUIN

Romance

A Christmas tradition...

Imagine spending Christmas in New
Orleans with a blind stranger and his aged
guide dog—when you're supposed to be
there on your honeymoon!
#3163 Every Kind of Heaven
by Bethany Campbell

Imagine spending Christmas with a man
you once "married"—in a mock ceremony
at the age of eight!
#3166 The Forgetful Bride
by Debbie Macomber

*Available in December 1991, wherever
Harlequin books are sold.*

RXM

"INDULGE A LITTLE" SWEEPSTAKES

HERE'S HOW THE SWEEPSTAKES WORKS

NO PURCHASE NECESSARY

To enter each drawing, complete the appropriate Official Entry Form or a 3" by 5" index card by hand-printing your name, address and phone number and the trip destination that the entry is being submitted for (i.e., Walt Disney World Vacation Drawing, etc.) and mailing it to: Indulge '91 Subscribers-Only Sweepstakes, P.O. Box 1397, Buffalo, New York 14269-1397.

No responsibility is assumed for lost, late or misdirected mail. Entries must be sent separately with first class postage affixed, and be received by: 9/30/91 for the Walt Disney World Vacation Drawing, 10/31/91 for the Alaskan Cruise Drawing and 11/30/91 for the Hawaiian Vacation Drawing. Sweepstakes is open to residents of the U.S. and Canada, 21 years of age or older as of 11/7/91.

For complete rules, send a self-addressed, stamped (WA residents need not affix return postage) envelope to: Indulge '91 Subscribers-Only Sweepstakes Rules, P.O. Box 4005, Blair, NE 68009.

DIR-RL

"INDULGE A LITTLE" SWEEPSTAKES

HERE'S HOW THE SWEEPSTAKES WORKS

NO PURCHASE NECESSARY

To enter each drawing, complete the appropriate Official Entry Form or a 3" by 5" index card by hand-printing your name, address and phone number and the trip destination that the entry is being submitted for (i.e., Walt Disney World Vacation Drawing, etc.) and mailing it to: Indulge '91 Subscribers-Only Sweepstakes, P.O. Box 1397, Buffalo, New York 14269-1397.

No responsibility is assumed for lost, late or misdirected mail. Entries must be sent separately with first class postage affixed, and be received by: 9/30/91 for the Walt Disney World Vacation Drawing, 10/31/91 for the Alaskan Cruise Drawing and 11/30/91 for the Hawaiian Vacation Drawing. Sweepstakes is open to residents of the U.S. and Canada, 21 years of age or older as of 11/7/91.

For complete rules, send a self-addressed, stamped (WA residents need not affix return postage) envelope to: Indulge '91 Subscribers-Only Sweepstakes Rules, P.O. Box 4005, Blair, NE 68009.

© 1991 HARLEQUIN ENTERPRISES LTD.

DIR-RL

INDULGE A LITTLE—WIN A LOT!

Summer of '91 Subscribers-Only Sweepstakes

OFFICIAL ENTRY FORM

This entry must be received by: Oct. 31, 1991
This month's winner will be notified by: Nov. 7, 1991
Trip must be taken between: May 27, 1992—Sept. 9, 1992
(depending on sailing schedule)

YES, I want to win the Alaska Cruise vacation for two. I understand the prize includes round-trip airfare, one-week cruise including private cabin, all meals and pocket money as revealed on the "wallet" scratch-off card.

Name _____

Address _____ Apt. _____

City _____

State/Prov. _____ Zip/Postal Code _____

Daytime phone number _____
(Area Code)

Return entries with invoice in envelope provided. Each book in this shipment has two entry coupons—and the more coupons you enter, the better your chances of winning!

© 1991 HARLEQUIN ENTERPRISES LTD.   2N-CPS

INDULGE A LITTLE—WIN A LOT!

Summer of '91 Subscribers-Only Sweepstakes

OFFICIAL ENTRY FORM

This entry must be received by: Oct. 31, 1991
This month's winner will be notified by: Nov. 7, 1991
Trip must be taken between: May 27, 1992—Sept. 9, 1992
(depending on sailing schedule)

YES, I want to win the Alaska Cruise vacation for two. I understand the prize includes round-trip airfare, one-week cruise including private cabin, all meals and pocket money as revealed on the "wallet" scratch-off card.

Name _____

Address _____ Apt. _____

City _____

State/Prov. _____ Zip/Postal Code _____

Daytime phone number _____
(Area Code)

Return entries with invoice in envelope provided. Each book in this shipment has two entry coupons—and the more coupons you enter, the better your chances of winning!

© 1991 HARLEQUIN ENTERPRISES LTD.   2N-CPS